Foreward

This novel is based on the fictitious murder of the Keeper family early in the 20th century. All of the characters, names and events in this book are fictitious, and any resemblance to actual persons, living or dead, is purely coincidental.

ISBN: 978-0-692-74862-6

With love and gratitude to my wife, children and family who have always shown me I could be more than I thought I could be.

Chapter 1

There it was; as it has always been. A sea of traffic comprised of both human and fuel-guzzling vehicles. A mass of stationery vehicles of every description and people who moved forward, sideward, and occasionally, at a strange angle. The traffic congestion has never gotten easier for those of us who must travel into and out of New York City, but as I looked east down 47th street past the groups of tourist following popsicle-holding tour guides around Times Square, I chuckled at the sea of yellow that marked this, and nearly every midtown street. Seems that driving a taxi in New York is a trial of one's patience beyond description. Ask why New Yorkers don't do something about it, and everyone has an opinion but never a solution. Previous government officials have taken mediocre steps to lessen the problem, but never seem to abate the situation.

Even on a spectacular day like today with the sun shinIng, gentle breezes blowing down the avenues, and a promised temperature approaching 56, did the congestion seem to be any more bearable. The only thing that would make me able to endure the traffic, pedestrians would be a good meeting with my publisher, Ben Haberman. Even on a spectacular day like today, Ben Haberman could not, would not, preach doom-and-gloom to me. Today was the first day of publication of my first novel. Even with Ben Haberman, congestion, people bumping and shoving and going every which way, today was a spectacular day. Yes, today was "A   OK"!

Funny that I would think of that term: 'A OK'. I had not used that term, or even thought about it in many, many years. It used to be the term which one of my 'roomies' used much too often while studying for tests in college.

Mike Rolden was not only a brilliant multi-major undergrad who shared a room with me and Shawn O'Leary, he was prone to repeat cute little sayings dozens of times a day. He claimed to have inherited that habit from his grandfather who used to say things like "if I had his money, and he had a feather, we would both be tickled", "it's a family thing", and, of course, "everything's A-OK!" We would be pulling all-nighters getting ready for exams, living on caffeine and more caffeine, and Mike would break the deadly silence with "don't worry, everything's A-OK!" Annoying as hell, but now it's ingrained in my subconscious forever.

About the time I saw my destination coming near on 44th street, a fast moving, don't-care-who's-in-my-way, type of fellow caught me full-on, at full speed and sent me flying backwards into people and the faux-marble façade of a building. After the sound of gasping, grunting and surprise from those people under me ended, I struggled to get back up on my feet. Not as easy as I thought it should be as I saw a slight tear in the arm of my suit. I knew that the tear would mean this suit would be heading for the 'donations' bag, never to be worn by me again. Oh, well, everything's A-OK.

On my feet and upright again, I gave hands and upper body strength to assist a middle age woman who seemed to still be in some shock back onto her feet. After confirming with her that she was fine, I surveyed the others who were in various stages of getting themselves up right and brushed off. Three business men, a young woman in her mid-thirties whose purple-and-green-dyed hair hardly matched her 'donations store' outfit, a freckled-face young man of probably twenty or twenty-one years of age, and a strikingly beautiful, model-type, blonde woman whose skirt was up way too high, revealing her pale green, Victoria's Secret micro panties, and much more of her than she would want to be seen.

After apologizing to everyone, and getting sympathetic "it wasn't your fault" responses, I looked down the street to see if the human freight train was still plowing through others. Not in sight. He had either made it around the corner, or ducked into one of the many doorways available.

As I attempted to help the young man clean the abrasions off his elbow with my handkerchief, the blonde told me I should get some medical attention right away for the cut on my forehead. It was about this time I felt the throbbing pain in my right shoulder meet the terrible headache coming forth as it met the feeling of a wet liquid slowing moving down my face. Apparently, as I fell backwards against the front of the building, I managed to fall onto an old, never-used-again, hose connection which was tougher than my 44-year-old skin. A deep gash made the right side of my face look as though I had been in a prize fight with the reigning champion, and lost badly. Swelling had already begun, and blood now dripped from my jaw down onto my 'donations bag' suit. Pain in my face was competing with the increasing pain in my shoulder as I wiped blood from my face.

As I cleaned off some blood, the middle-age woman stepped forward and identified herself as "Dr. Helen Eldon", an on-staff surgeon at Mount Sinai Hospital. She quickly opened her black bag, which I took to be a large purse, and took out some antiseptic pads, gauze, tape and three-to-four butterfly bandages. As she expertly cleaned my wound, others said their farewells and departed. The young man tried to collect various sheets of paper that he and I had dropped from our hands upon impact, and sorted through them to see which ones belonged to whom. As he took his papersand replaced them into a folder he had, he handed others to me with a hope that everything was there. I thanked him as Dr. Eldon placed the final butterfly bandage over my wound, and asked him if he wanted the doctor to check his abrasions and elbows.

"No, thank you", he said, "I've got to get back to work, I'm late already." And with that, he quickly darted on down the street dodging the oncoming bodies.

"Here is my card. If you are close by Mount Sinai, stop in to have further attention given to your injuries. Or, if you need me to refer you to a physician for follow up, contact me. You need to see someone for additional medical attention. Also, you will have a pretty good 'shiner' in a couple hours that will require looking at. Your injuries, while not life-threatening, are more serious than you may think. Get a doctor to examine you at first opportunity," said Dr. Eldon.

I thanked her again as she picked up remaining items and put them back into her large, black handbag. I offered to pay her for her time and the items she had used, but she said "no", waved me off and began walking away down the street.

So much for a spectacular day.

I put my batch of papers back into my brief bag and headed on to Ben Haberman's office.

While it was not one of New York's most spectacular buildings, Sorrabon Publishing's inner offices were. Sorrabon had taken their money and spent in on the inside where employees and clients would appreciate it more than a newly-cleaned, somewhat updated building front on 44th. They polished old brass pieces to the point that one could almost shave with them. They installed marble where marble could best be seen and appreciated. They hired craftsmen to panel, polish, and create wooden walls that were, at times, beyond belief. Yes, Sorrabon Publishing had come to the U.S from

Europe with money, people, and technology necessary to make a statement and impact in the publishing field. They had acquired several older, large U.S. publishing firms and took their best and brightest minds and formed the new publishing company. With seemingly unlimited capital, bright minds, who knew their craft, and some good writers as clients, they became a mega-conglomerate in just a couple years. MSNBC and the folks at Bloomberg speculated that Sorrabon had done to the publishing business what Comcast had done to TV broadcasting: gotten huge! And, they had done it in only two years! There were also rumors in the business world that Sorrabon was looking to expand into areas of media and other businesses. Good Luck! I thought. Having been a small businessman for many years, and gone through the pangs of growth and such, I knew it was not as easy as they had had it so far.

Getting into 1735 44th Street was not as simple as opening a door and entering. First you pressed a button, then you answered "Yes, who is it?" from the speaker mounted high above the door. You then give your name and person you want to see. After a couple minutes, the front door automatically opens and you walk into a sort of reception room of about 250 square feet. A room furnished only with six straight-back wooden chairs and a small plain table in the middle. From here you give all your worldly possessions to a guard behind a large, bullet proof window, and proceed through the first of two metal detectors. Yes. Two metal detectors. People have said that it is easier to get into the Pentagon than it is to get inside Sorrabon Publishing.

Having retrieved my worldly possessions, I walked to the three elevators nearby and waited. Oh, did I mention Sorrabon's technology? After about ten seconds, a very nice female voice asked me "Going up, or down, sir?" What would she have said if I were not a sir?

"Going up, seventh floor. Ben Haberman," I replied.

"Thank you, sir. Please enter now, and exit at the rear when reaching the seventh floor. And, sir, have a fabulous day." was the response from the hidden voice.

The door opened, I entered. Within a matter of seconds we were at the seventh floor and the hidden voice said, "Mr. Ben Haberman's office is on the left, sir." With that I exited. Isn't technology great!

Before I could take more than a couple steps down the teak wood paneled hallway, Ben was rushing out his office door.

"What the hell happened?" Ben shouted at me. "I heard you got mugged on 44th!"

I sort of chuckled to myself at the word 'mugged'. "No, not mugged," I answered. "Just some fool in a mega hurry and decided to knock over half dozen, or so, pedestrians."

"You look like hell, and you have quite the black eye there. Our security department saw it happen and said it looked like a mugging of several people. They didn't know that one of them was a client of ours or they would have caught the guy," Ben added as he grabbed my hand to shake it.

Shaking hands with Ben sent waves of searing pain up and down my arm and had my right shoulder throbbing even more. I thought about taking a moment and downing a couple of Advil tablets, but decided just to concentrate on getting this meeting over with and finding a martini with my name on it.

Apparently the pain I experienced showed on my face as Ben stopped trying to shake my hand and apologized for any discomfort.

"Come into my office, sit down, relax and I'll get us a couple drinks going," Ben instructed. He knew the shortcut to my heart with "a couple drinks" offer. Hope he didn't plan to have any.

Ben's office was typical for an upper level executive manager at Sorrabon Publishing. He had the normal 'enter-thru-this-main-door' door, a beautiful, leggy, brunette secretary, the 'let's escape through this secret 'back door' door, and all the comforts that any human could imagine. Ben also had a glass-walled office on three sides. A glass-walled office on three sides; yes, the fourth side was your standard wall which was part of the teak wood paneled hallway. What fascinated me about Ben's office was that when he wanted privacy, as when he was with a client, Ben flipped a switch under his desk and the glass went from clear, see-through walls, to a completely translucent wall on each of the three sides. Light would continue to filter through, but no clear images or details could be seen. Along with this translucency, a series of tones, or sounds, encompassed Ben's office so that conversations, or any sound made, could not be heard outside the office walls. Did I mention Sorrabon's technology?

By the time we got through the 'secret' door into Ben's office, Ben's secretary Veronica was standing there holding two martinis. I would have downed both of them, given the chance, but Veronica set one on Ben's desk and offered me the second one. As Veronica started out the other office door, she told me that my martini was my favorite French vodka and was made 'dirty'. With that she lightly giggled and left Ben's office.

As we both sat down, Ben offered up a toast, "Here's to better days for you, and bigger checks for us both". We both took a big, long sip of our superbly-made martinis and sighed.

"Bigger checks for us both?" I asked. Any check, at this point has to be bigger because I've not gotten check one.

"Bigger than what?" I asked Ben, realizing that I had nearly finished the martini.

"Oh, yeah. By the way, here is your first author's check from us," was Ben's reply as he handed me a piece of folded paper.

As I opened it, my jaw must have dropped down to the floor below. "What is this all about," I asked. "I thought the book went to press today, and that means no copies sold yet."

Ben leaned back in his over-stuffed, executive chair and smiled. "Hidden somewhere deep in your contract is our right to 'pre-publish' and distribute any novels outside the U.S. before we commence publishing here in the States. We did that and your novel went, shall I use the term Platinum, in Europe. That check is from those sales. We expect it to do even better here in the States."

As I gazed at the numbers on the check, I had to count zeros to determine just how big the check really was. "Why wasn't I made aware that this was being done?" I asked.

"Do you really want to quibble over pre-publishing rights, or have another drink to celebrate?" Ben asked, as the office door opened and Veronica brought me another 'dirty' martini. "If you doubt what I'm telling you regarding pre-publishing rights, go home and read your copy of our contract. It's in there somewhere. I let the legal beagles worry about that, I just give the 'yay', or nay. It's the 'yay' that brings you that check," Ben added.

"I don't doubt what you're telling me, Ben, it's just so surprising to me to receive a check of this size. I thought that, maybe, just maybe, if my first novel was good, that I might get this much money after novels one and two. Not from Europe. Pleasantly surprised, that's all."

"Well, you are a brilliant writer, and as long as you can keep creating, like you did on number one, we both will be getting bigger checks. Now, down to business," Ben said as he turned to remove several folders from a side filing cabinet. "Where are you on book two?" he asked. "Do you have the outline drafted yet?"

"Yes, I do, but I'll need a few minutes to reassemble my pages that spilled out onto the sidewalk when the freight train hit me earlier. I'll do that now and give you my copy."

"Okay, I'll need that copy for a meeting tomorrow morning. I can return it after that. If it's as good as book one, you're swimming in honey!"

Honey? "Honey?" I asked, "It doesn't really sound that inviting to swim in." I continued to rearrange the various page numbers until I had everything in order, then handed the batch to Ben. I was really having a lot of pain in my shoulder and my face was beginning to hurt more, and more.

Ben looked through the various pages without saying a word. Finally, he smiled and put all the papers into a folder on his desk. He leaned back in his chair, stared at the ceiling and said "I think it's time to lose the privacy in this office, and I have to get ready for an upcoming meeting. You need to see yourself out." And with that Ben flipped his hidden switch and like magic the foggy walls became crystal clear again and showed a myriad of people rushing about in the outer office.

I may not have a genius IQ, but I know when it's time for my exit. I folded my check, picked up the remains of my brief bag and downed the last drops of my martini. As I walked through Ben's inner office door, I heard Ben say, "Thanks, and I'll call you in a couple days to go over number one and how we stand on book two."

As I walked out of the building into bright sunshine I wondered what to do first, whether to go back to my apartment and change or to go deposit the check.

The check won.

I quickly walked three blocks to a branch of my bank and went straight to a teller's window. She was busy counting currency and completely ignored me while I repeatedly cleared my throat and tapped my fingernails on her marble shelf. When she had counted the last of her currency, she looked up at me with one eyebrow raised and asked, "Can I help you with something?"

I smiled and replied that I wanted to deposit this check

into my account. I handed the folded piece of paper to her and watched her as her eyes got larger and larger. She excused herself for a moment and took my check to a man seated at a large desk behind her. The two talked to each other as if discussing a secret and turned occasionally to look, and smile, at me. Finally the man got up from his desk and walked toward me with the teller following close behind. While the man was polite in speaking to me, he was also adamant in quoting the bank's policies regarding checks of a certain size.

"I fully understand that there will be a hold put on some of the funds," I explained to the man. "I simply want it deposited so that nothing happens to it since this has not been one of my best days."

"I'm not one to judge, sir, but I would have guessed that today may not have gone as you planned," the bank man said. With that said, he had me endorse the check, sign the deposit slip, and after a few minutes handed me a receipt for my deposit.

As I exited the bank building and turned into the mass of people still moving this way, that way, and a couple of other directions, I looked at the shadows now being cast upon everything by the soon-to-be-setting sun and thought to myself "What a spectacular day!"

CHAPTER 2

It wasn't the world's biggest, loudest, or most expensive celebration; it wasn't as if we had just won a world war and had invited all the victorious countries to join with us. It definitely was very large, very boisterous, and expensive enough for me and my checkbook. My fiancé, Stephanie Walker, thought it was 'modest and tastefully done.'

We had just announced our engagement publicly to 160 of our closest friends and family. Yes, it was to be a small, little 'get together' of 40 or 50 people, tops. A luncheon, and open bar reminded me of how expensive some things in life can be. Engagements? Yes! Weddings? Yes! Honeymoons? Yes! Daily living in greater New England? Yes! Marrying into the Walker family? Most definitely! For Stephanie comes from good stock. Banking and financial stock; people that include Stock Market people which made her family one of the more notable families in New England. She was used to the very best and her father told me once that I had better "not try to give her city water; she was used to champagne." So noted.

The Walker family was old, established money and watched their world, and most everyone else's world very closely. They were never short of words. Especially words of criticism. Criticism that seemed to be as abundant as breaths of air. The family watched Stephanie's second marriage, to Aaron Vanderkline, so closely that Stephanie once joked to me that she had to ask her mother once if she and Aaron had had sex the night before, as she had fallen asleep.

This is not to imply that there were not advantages to being part of the Walker family. There definitely were. Besides Stephanie, who was a very successful Manhattan attorney, there was her father who controlled much of Wall Street's trading activity, a brother, Carl, who was Senior VP of Citicorp, brother Andrew, who was vice president of one of the country's largest precious metals trading firms, and sister, Andrea, who was a top physicist, and was set on saving the world. The 'black sheep' of the Walker family was the youngest son, Gerald, who was 'only' a doctor specializing in family practice. Gerald, or Gerry as the family referred to him, was not held in high esteem by Mr. & Mrs. Walker and considered somewhat of an under-achiever. He was happily married with three children, a beautiful loving wife, a nice, large home in Rhode Island, and a large, very successful family practice. Underachiever? Sometimes I wondered what they really thought of me as a soon-to-be son-in-law who was only a highly successful author. What's below the rung of an underachiever?

Stephanie had already proven her value, as my attorney, as she renegotiated my author's contract with Sorrabon Publishing getting nearly double the money-per-book, not to mention many other favorable things that benefited us. She was somewhat ruthless when dealing with Ben Haberman and the other top managers, and she always said that discussing, or negotiating contracts was not meant for the faint of heart. Now with this team on my side it was easy to sit and concentrate on book six.

"Sir, is there anything else that we can do for you before we clean up," was the question that brought me out of my short day dream. The maître'd had stopped directing his 'army' of people to ask me if I was able to think of something else that I needed, or wanted.

"No. Thank you for an excellent job and my compliments to your entire staff" I replied.

"I'm almost embarrassed to ask this of you, sir" he continued as he held out a copy of my lastest book. "My wife is one of your biggest fans and missed seeing you at your book signing in West Chester last month. She read your book and would be so honored if you would sign it for her. Am I stepping out of line, sir?"

"Absolutely not; you are not the least bit out of line and I would be happy to sign it." I reached into my inside jacket pocket to retrieve a pen, and asked, "What would you like it to say?"

"Her name is Marilyn, and anything you think of, would be great." With that he smiled and let me open the front cover to begin. As I wrote how thankful I was for loyal fans like Marilyn, and thanked her for her good taste in literature, I wished her and her family good health and good fortune, I promised Marilyn my next novel would be even better than the previous ones. As I wrote, I reminded myself how fortunate I was for what my life had become.

"When you're done with that, we need to leave. Mother and Daddy will be meeting us at the restaurant shortly and we do not want to keep Daddy waiting," Stephanie said as she walked past me sitting at a table signing Marilyn's book.

I watched her walk off to meet two sorority sisters and go, arm-in-arm, into an adjoining banquet room. Beautiful lady, I thought. Beautiful, successful, fun-loving, and soon to become my wife. Her first two marriages had not gone well at all. The first marriage to a physically-abusive, alcoholic husband, ended after just six months. Marriage number two lasted two years plus, and ended when Stephanie and her husband found out that she was incapable of ever having children. Now she was willing to give love and marriage another try. I was very thankful for that fact and wanted for both of us to be happy and to grow old together laughing.

Her two sorority sisters were part of the 100 or so 'extras' we had at our small, 40 person luncheon. Yes, we were going to have a small group of immediate family, close personal friends, and close business associates. Then we added more friends, and a couple more, and a few more. Suddenly, as with many get-togethers, we were straining the seating capacity of the restaurant. But, that was over now and we were off to have dinner with "Mother and Daddy."

I finished signing the book, handed it back to the man in the spotless tuxedo, thanked him again for everything and walked onward to catch up with Stephanie. I looked around the closed restaurant and wondered what kind of evening dinner people they would soon see. Movie goers? Couples heading off to see the latest, greatest Broadway plays? Music lovers, who were apt to spend an evening at one of the many concerts available this evening? As I neared the front entrance I saw Stephanie giving final hugs and kisses to her sorority sisters. I returned their waves of goodbye and gave serious thought to possibly blowing them a kiss goodbye. Best not. Don't know how Stephanie would interpret that if she saw it.

As we stepped into our taxi, a loud voice called out from somewhere. It was Ben Haberman rushing toward us. He was trying to get my attention before we left to get an update on my current novel. Seems he had a meeting early in the morning and I would be a topic of first discussion. Ben, with all his positives, was not a relaxed, calm individual.

"A great get-together, you two. Thank you so much for including my wife and I," Ben said as he held the taxi door open and peered inside. "What can I tell everyone at the meeting tomorrow morning?"

I smiled at nervous Ben and said, "tell them that I am two-thirds done and they will see a published novel before the due date." I adjusted my seat belt and added, "and tell them that this will be my best book ever!"

After Ben gently closed my door and thanked me profusely, the driver asked for the address and drove off.

The early evening sky was clouded over and seemed as though rain was eminent. The evening temps would not require an overcoat, but I wore one from habit anyway. I watched each building and group of people go by in a blur, and almost didn't hear what Stephanie was saying to me.

"Did you hear me?" she asked. "I think you still need to put more distance between yourself and Ben Haberman. He is not the friend that you think him to be." She poked me in the side and smiled as she added, "If fact, it may be time to move beyond Sorrabon Publishing for future works. Don't you agree?"

"Ben and Sorrabon have been very good to me over the years, and I don't think I would find a better fit than them," I answered. The taxi had only gone four blocks before more typical New York City traffic forced us into maximum speeds of between ten and fifteen miles-per-hour. The buildings and people were no longer blurs. We moved at a pure 'stop-and-no go' pace for several blocks before I suggested to Stephanie that we abandon the taxi and walk the rest of the way. She hesitated saying something about her new dress just not suitable for rain or pigeons. I reminded her how her "Daddy" would be at dinner if we were late meeting them, and what an uncomfortable evening it would be for others. She sighed loudly, smiled, and agreed that exiting might be best.

As we left the taxi, Stephanie was again asking me about Ben Haberman and Sorrabon Publishing. I tried to get her to think more about getting to the restaurant on time and about other, higher priority items.

"Let's concentrate on dinner tonight, the wedding plans, and, don't forget, we still need to buy a house to live in. Ben and Sorrabon can be topics of discussion later," I said, as I saw the front of the restaurant come into view. The doorman recognized us immediately and opened the door with a huge smile saying, "good evening Mr. & Mrs. Walker. How are you two?" We both laughed to ourselves after telling him we were fine and dropped our coats at the check room.

There in a semi-private, side room was the Walker family. Besides the 'other' Mr. & Mrs. Walker, sat Andrea and her husband, and the Walker's son, Carl, and his wife. The spouses of the Walker siblings were 'different'. Andrea's husband was a research biologist who always seemed to be off in another world; at least in another time zone. Carl's wife, on the other hand, is a chemical engineer, and researcher, who always wanted to run some type of analysis on her water, and every bit of food in front of her. Bet she was a fun one at a cocktail party. But, I could be the underachiever of this group, so I tried to be nice to all and find something to talk about with Andrea's husband. "Good luck with that," I told myself as Mr. Walker greeted Stephanie and I at the table.

Mrs. Walker asked me to sit next to her on the far side of the table, which left Stephanie to sit next to her brother, Carl. I started to go pull Stephanie's chair out for her, as a New York gentleman should do, but saw that a waiter already had done so and was holding her linen napkin in his hand.

As I sat down in my spot at the table, Mrs. Walker asked where I get all the ideas for my novels. She said she could not imagine a head being so full of so many different ideas at the same time. I tried to explain that as I am researching for one novel, sometimes an idea or thought for a completely different story line will come to mind. I write down some notes, or make a recording of the items that I want to build upon, and that is part of the foundation of another story. Once in a while, as was the case between books three and five, notes I made from researching Egyptian archeological findings came to mind in the middle of the night in the form of a complete story line. I got up and started typing. Twelve hours later I had the draft outline done along with the first four chapters of book four. Book four was my most successful novel until book eight was published.

Mr. Walker thanked everyone for clearing their calendars

for tonight's dinner. He felt that, with everyone's busy schedules, that fewer and fewer dinners with the family would be possible for he and his wife. With that being said, he seemed to stare off to the left corner of the ceiling and take a few seconds to compose himself. He then made a toast to Stephanie and I, wishing us much happiness and welcoming me, again, into the family. He then announced that he had taken the liberty of pre-ordering dinner, and knew that everyone would be happy with his selection. This part of the announcement did not seem to sit well with Carl's wife, Carla. What? I never thought of it before: Carl and Carla! Wait a minute! Not only did we have a Carl and Carla combo, but I was fairly certain that Andrea's husband's name was Andrew. Andrea and Andrew, Carl and Carla, now things were getting strange. I began to wonder what brother-in-law Andrew's wife's name was. Agnes maybe? Abigail? My creative side of my brain was running amuck with possibilities when I heard Andrea ask me about a wedding date.

"Nothing is firm, yet. We're trying to get everyone's calendars meshed together, and to find a time for the priest and church. Plus we have to think about a place to live in as neither Steph's apartment, nor mine would be large enough for two people." Having said that, Andrea corrected me with "Stephanie. My sister's name is Stephanie!" I looked at her for a moment, then asked if she and her husband had shortened, more personal names for each other. Or, did they prefer cute nicknames?

"We both have names given to us at birth by our parents. Loving, caring parents. We use those names. There is no need for, as you call them, nicknames!" The look on Andrea's face told me that I had made a major blunder. At least with her it was.

"To each it's own," I replied. "Some people like nicknames, others do not. I found in some of my research, that many ancient societies had nicknames for people who were close, or special. Some going back as far as 100 BC."

"We are not ancient, we are civilized. Civilized people use correct terms or names." With that statement, Andrea turned to her other side to talk with her husband. Well, one in-law mad at me, how would the rest of the dinner fare?

"You said you were looking for a place for you and Stephanie to live in?" was the question directed to me. I turned to see a smiling Carla leaning forward onto the table. "House? Condo? Apartment?" she asked.

"Would prefer a house; a fairly large house, as I need an office for my work. Stephanie needs an office, also for when she must work at home. So, I just don't see an apartment or condo being large enough for us. Steph, err Stephanie, would love an old, well maintained, Victorian-type place with a huge front porch and four or five bedrooms. Big house on a big lot would be great."

Carla continued smiling, and seemed to ponder her next statement for a few seconds before adding "my brother has a fraternity brother who is tops in residential real estate. He is partnered with one of the largest firms in all the Northeast. Perhaps he can be of some help."

"That would be appreciated. We don't seem to have as much time as we would like. Regardless of the wedding date, and such, we need to concentrate on finding a suitable, affordable house in a good location. We have discussed several areas, but Stephanie would prefer Massachusetts or Connecticut. I don't know what areas this fellow works in but would appreciate talking with him."

"As soon as I can get Carl away from talking investments and money with his father, I'll talk to him about it. Hope his friend can help in some way." Carla said with her ear-to-ear smile.

Well, I thought to myself, the evening is a tie. One in-law mad at me and not talking to me, and one in-law smiling at me and offering to help find a house. Let's see how the rest of the evening goes.

The dinner was its' usual fabulous self. Great salad, with the Chef's secret dressing lightly drizzled on it. A superb cut of meat with everything else just magically prepared and beautifully presented. The chatter was light and non-condemning from Andrea and the others, and the wine selection matched everyone's taste and liking.

After thanking the Walkers, and the others, for a most enjoyable evening, I retrieved our coats and helped Stephanie on with hers.

We decided that the faint mist coming down was not a good enough reason to prevent our walking back to Stephanie's apartment. At least walking most of the way back. If the mist got heavier, or turned into full fledged rain, we would taxi it the rest of the way.

As we walked, we talked about wedding items, guest list, upcoming schedules for both of us, and I related my blunder with Andrea. Stephanie sided with Andrea, somewhat, with pretty much the same line of logic Andrea used: parents give us names to be used, not chopped up and shortened. Okay, better leave that topic for another time, I thought. Don't ask her if I can call her 'Steph'. I also told her about the fraternity brother of Carla's brother, and how Carla said he was an outstanding residential real estate agent in some of the areas we were interested in looking at.

"I would love to see homes in the Bridgeport or New Haven coastal areas," she said as we slowed to a stop in front of her brownstone apartment building. "We could get a boat and spend our huge amount of free time just relaxing as we sail off the coast." Sailing. Relaxing. Words which didn't seem to translate into words which described our hectic schedules lately. "If he can help us find a house, that would be great and would take one more item off our plates."

I agreed and told her that I would follow up with Carla. After a warm embrace and "good night's," I hailed a taxi to continue on my way home.

The taxi arrived just as the heavier rain started falling. You would think that, by now, I would know when to carry an umbrella. I don't, but the taxi would drop me at the front of my apartment building and I would make a mad dash for the front door hoping to run in between falling drops of rain.

It happened just the way I said it would.

Not!

The taxi made good time until we got within three blocks of my apartment. At that point we were held in place by some sort of police action somewhere down a cross street. Minutes ticked off the meter and we didn't move. More time elapsed and still we sat in the same spot just three blocks from home.

Finally, after an additional eighteen dollars had ticked off the meter, and we had not moved a foot, I paid the driver and got out. Second mistake of my evening.

The weather person on the late news reported it as a 'historic amount of rain,' all of which fell entirely within the block that I live in. Every drop; every ounce of liquid hit me and drenched me right through my clothes and into my skin. By the time I had reached my apartment, I swore that I would never feel dry ever again. Now, where did I put those umbrellas?

CHAPTER 3

Carla's brother, Johnny Hamilton is a branch manager for a regional banking firm, and manages their largest branch in Albany, New York. Johnny's fraternity brother, Howard Wilkins, was every bit as good as we hoped he would be. He knew the areas, knew the market, and, once Stephanie told him that we did not have a budgeted amount for our home, Howard really became ignited with energy. Her father's saying of "don't try to give her city water, she is used to champagne" kept running through my head. Over a span of six weeks he showed us everything from adorable four bedroom colonials, to estate-sized custom built, large square footage homes. Many were nice, but just not the right one, according to Stephanie. Every house lacked one, or more, key things that Stephanie felt her dream house needed.

Howard showed us more than 22 homes from the Port Chester area of Connecticut, all the way up I-95 to Bridgeport. We were more than tired of looking, and not getting calendar dates, guest lists, and other wedding related items done. We were almost to the point of quitting when Howard phoned.

"I have just gotten off the phone with a friend of mine who knows of a Victorian Mansion in Westport that will be going on the market soon. It has almost five thousand square feet of space, has six bedrooms, six and a half baths, a gourmet kitchen with all new stainless appliances, a library and two offices. It sits right on the water and has its' own dock, boat lift and boat house."

It has a three and a half car garage, but is very close to the train station if you want to commute to the city." Howard took a moment to catch his breath before continuing with "it has been restored and is in pristine condition. I have photos of it if you would like me to email them to you."

"Please do. You have my email address. I'll look at them and if it is as nice as you say, I'll show Stephanie tonight when I see her."

"There's only..." Howard was saying as the connection went from fairly good to horrible. Static and intermittent dead silence came between the few words of his conversation. "...owned the grocery store...the roofing...custom designed and built for them. It's unfortunate that...wife and children...loved..." And with that Howard went completely silent.

It was almost an hour later before the email from Howard arrived in my 'in basket' and I viewed the photos. Without a doubt this Victorian mansion has everything we are looking for, and more. I couldn't believe the beauty of it. Huge bedrooms, lavish bathrooms, a chef-quality kitchen with large food prep areas. Two offices almost custom designed for Stephanie and I. It seemed too good to be true. The boat house and dock were over sized for anything that we might have in our flotilla. But the entire property was just unbelievable. Just about everything that Stephanie and I could want in our home was plainly visible in these photos; and everything looked to be in brand new, or near-new condition. Nothing was missing.

How was the wi-fi, I wondered? Probably the one negative that could squelch any potential deal as both of us have to have high speed connections in order to do our work. Well, I would find out, that was for certain! I would not let weak wi-fi, or low signal strength, stop this. I'll need to print copies of the main photos to take to dinner with me. The rest I would send to my iPhone in case Stephanie wanted to see all the pictures.

Printing completed, I grabbed my topcoat and umbrella and headed to the phone to summon a taxi. It could be an exciting dinner tonight.

The driver did his best to maneuver through the traffic, but everything was against him. And me. He threatened once to turn and drive down the extra wide sidewalk, but it, too, was congested and slow-moving. He murmured under his breath and let out a low pitched whistle when he was able to finally get the taxi above twenty-miles-per-hour. After that he was outwardly happier.

The restaurant was packed, but, fortunately, Stephanie had made a reservation for us so no waiting would be necessary. As

I was shown to our table, which was without any Stephanie, I noticed the 'dirty' martini sitting waiting for me. I asked if this drink belonged to someone. I was told that Ms. Stephanie had preordered it to be ready upon my arrival, and they hoped it was to my liking. There was only one way to answer that question.

It was twenty minutes later, and another martini, that Stephanie came rushing in. Looking as though she had just run several blocks, she grabbed me and gave me a hug and kiss on the cheek. She said she was sorry for not meeting me here on time but that her court case had gone much longer on cross examination than it should have. She sat down opposite me and took her drink that had been set in front of her in her hand to raise as a toast.

"Here's to many more dinners together without being late," she said. "And to love and to growing old together."

We lightly tapped our glasses together as I echoed her toast and asked how her court case seemed to be heading. I sipped the liquid in my glass as I vaguely listened to the 'ifs' and 'maybe's' of the case. Seems as though her client, a well respected, and world famous, female fashion designer had 'accidentally' killed her wife while fixing dinner one evening. Stephanie's task was to show that the stab wound in her neck, which severed her carotid artery, had in fact been an accident. The more that Stephanie talked about her client's fashions, and her stores in Paris, London, Berlin, and Milan, Italy, the more it sounded like her client could possibly be guilty. Occasionally I would smile and nod my head as we watched our dinners being presented before us.

Finally Stephanie paused and asked how the book was progressing.

"Before I forget," Stephanie continued, not giving me a chance to answer her about the book, "Carla has agreed to be a bridesmaid, and I finally got a response from my sorority sister, Karen Benton. She will also. So I have my posse put together. How are you doing?"

I smiled and asked which question she wanted answered first. The book, or the posse? Seems the posse, at this moment, was much more important. "I'm all set. My brother, Nathan, and some homeless guy named Guido." Then there was the stare, blank expression, and complete silence from her for what seemed to be five minutes. Slowly a smile formed on her lips as she said, "and some homeless guy named Guido?"

I laughed, nearly choking on a sample of crab cake. "I thought I might try to reach out to help the less fortunate." There were many moments in our relationship that Stephanie did not understand, or appreciate, my sense of humor. This must be another one.

"Seriously, how are you doing?" she asked. "We are

coming down to the wire with wedding items and we need to get more checked off our lists."

"Seriously," I replied, "everything is fine. Relax. My brother Nathan is on board, and Guido, my close friend from grad school, will also be a groomsman. The male side of the altar is ready and they have already been to fittings for their tuxedos."

"You have talked about Guido before, but have I ever met him?"

"You met him two years ago at the Governor's Ball," I answered. "He is the taller, extremely handsome fellow who had his arm in a sling because of a hunting accident in Africa. The fellow who kept saying how much he loved your eyes and smile."

"Oh yes," she laughed, "the guy who I had to keep telling that both my smile and eyes were up here, not where he was looking. I remember Guido. Does Guido have a last name?"

"Kiefer," I replied. "He was the Mayor of Hartford, Connecticut, and rumored to be the first choice for the Republican ticket for state governor in next year's election." I finished my dinner and ordered another martini. Besides being one of our favorite restaurants for food, they had the best bartenders when it came to mixing martinis. Any type, Gin or Vodka, and any style, Yuri always made to perfection. Stephanie agreed and always loved getting together for quick, informal dinners here, especially when those dinners were just the two of us.

"Guido and Kiefer don't seem to go together. I would assume that Guido is Italian, but Kiefer would not be" she remarked. She had a puzzled look on her face as she placed her knife across her fork on her plate of unfinished food. "Do you know anything about his background? Where is he from? What is his family like? Is he married?"

"Wait! Wait," I interjected into Stephanie's stream of questions. "He's my friend and will be one of my groomsmen, he is not on trial here. Why is all of this important? Where is all this coming from?"

"Sorry, love, I didn't mean to step on toes, but I find the pairing of Guido and Kiefer to be less of a match, than a match. Just curious. Just curious."

We finished sharing a dessert, and our drinks, before reviewing other wedding items. The flowers? Check. The priest was available on what dates? Check this out. The list of guests? Still had to put more work into that one. Seems like we have more 'to dos' than we thought.

"When can we meet with Howard Wilkins to see the house in Westport?," I asked Stephanie.

"What house in Westport?" Stephanie replied. It was then I

realized that with nearly an hour and a half of conversation between us, I had not mentioned the house that Howard and I had talked about earlier that day. Nor, had I shown Stephanie the photos I printed off before leaving for our dinner engagement.

"I'm sorry", I said taking copies of photos out of my inner coat pocket. "Howard called me all excited about this house that was going to go on the market soon, and he thought it was perfect for us. He gave me all the particulars during some in-and-out, poor quality, cell phone conversing and later sent me an email with photos. Far too many pictures to print in their entirety, but I did print off these." I handed the stack of pictures to Stephanie and looked for our waiter.

Stephanie's eyes kept getting bigger and bigger. Finally, she looked across the table at me as I ordered another martini, and said, "This is unbelievable. Simply unbelievable!" Her eyes were welling up with tears which she wiped away with the back of her hand. "It's as if...I can't believe that this house actually exists! It's as if someone looked at our entire list of wants and wishes, and built a mansion according to our list. I can't believe this!" With that, she let out a long, silent sigh and smiled at me.

"Sorry it took all evening to get to this point. Seems like we get talking about our businesses, then wedding plans, then Guido came into the conversations, and I forgot about this house. I take it from your reaction that you might be interested in seeing it?" I took one long sip of my martini and tried to remember what number it was. Three? Five? Don't know. Maybe I'll finish this one and have some extra strong coffee. Somehow, I had to get up from this chair and walk like a sober person when Stephanie was ready to leave.

"Interested? I would go right this minute if we could," Stephanie added. "What a beautiful find this one is. Did Howard say how much?"

"Not that I heard. I think he may have been in a bad transmit area of the city because the last three to four minutes of our conversation I could only hear a couple, three words at a time. He kept cutting out and finally just disappeared. So I can't say he did, or did not, give me the price. But price aside, we need to meet with Howard and tour the house. As soon as we can before anyone learns of its' availability."

Stephanie was already looking at her calendar on her iPhone and had a frown on her face. "I'm in court tomorrow and Friday morning. Then I have a meeting with Amy Vanderbilt which cannot be changed. I've been trying to get her to bring the family legal affairs to my firm for years, and I think she is finally ready to make the move. Can we do something first thing Saturday morning?"

"I'll see. I'll call Howard in the morning and see if that is doable. Hopefully, no one else is aware of the house being available, and we can close something quickly if you really like it. We may need a good attorney," I added, "Do you happen to know of one?"

Stephanie laughed politely, still slowly moving her head from side-to-side in disbelief. "I'll see if I can locate a 'good attorney' while you set up a house tour, mister." She asked to keep the photos to show her sister tomorrow when they met for their monthly 'dinner on the green'.

CHAPTER 4

Connecticut seemed to have something for everyone; it least in the late Spring, Summer, and early Fall months. Winter months could be brutal, especially along the coastal towns. The state is a mix of coastal cities and rural areas dotted with small towns. Beluga whales could still be seen in early Spring right off the coastline as they showed their young ones the abundance of food between Fisher's Island, near New London, and the much colder waters of Grand Manan Island, New Brunswick. Famed for its seaports filled with centuries-old ships, The city of New Haven is home to one of the more notable ivy-league colleges, Yale University.

Connecticut is a haven for every type of yachting club one could imagine. Nearly every weekend was consumed with competitive sailings and contests between this yacht club, and that one; competition which was taken extremely serious. Competition which I hoped to become part of one day. If you didn't own a boat, even a small, single sail skiff, people had to know why you would live in Connecticut.

Saturday was beautiful with only small, white puffy clouds interrupting the clear blue sky. The sun was out, but was not overly warm. Comfortable, I thought; freezing, thought Stephanie.

Howard Wilkins met us in the parking lot at a diner he

chose which was just off the interstate highway, and easy to find. Howard has one of those old, classic 'E Class' Mercedes cars that I wished I owned. Genuine wood panel interior, and interior fabric that looked as new as the day it was installed. Roomy and comfortable was our drive to Westport to see the house.

"Where were you when you called me about the house?" I asked Howard. "You sounded like you were on your cell phone, but the connection was very poor."

"Sorry about that," answered Howard, "I was in Hartford, looking up some old deeds for another client. No reason to have a poor connection that I can think of." Howard slowed to make a left turn onto a road marked as "Private Property, No Trespassing."

"Maybe it was sun spots, or something," he continued. "Hopefully you received the email okay and the 'pics' were good enough quality to make out the fine details of each room, as well as the exterior."

"Email and photos were fine, thank you," I answered as we turned onto Stony Point Road and traveled alongside the Saugatuck River for several hundred yards. I didn't hear the harps play, or the angels' trumpets sound, but I could tell from the muted gasp coming from Stephanie in the front seat that we had arrived.

I believe Howard's car had stopped by the time Stephanie bolted from it, but I can't say for certain. She stood there alongside the Mercedes just looking at the white and dark-green trimmed exterior which seemed almost to blind us in the mid-morning sunlight. She stared at it forever before turning to me with tears in her eyes and saying, "Let's buy it! Now!"

Laughing, I told her I thought we should see if there was an interior before making an offer.

Howard excused himself to answer a phone call, and Stephanie and I proceeded inside.

As stunning and gorgeous as the grounds in front were, and the exterior of the home is, the entryway is even more so. It had a large, curving staircase which wound up to the second, and then onward to the third floor. Beautiful dark oak and walnut bannisters and stairs took one away from the large foyer which lead off to the left and right to other rooms. Every room, so far, was better, more beautiful than the previous room had been. There was nothing wrong with any room, any space. Every step seemed to take Stephanie's breath away. Stephanie and I had completed our tour of the third floor, and were halfway through all rooms on the second level when Howard found us.

"My apologies, folks, an urgent call from my father's doctor regarding a medical matter. Hope you're able to find your way around okay. The house is a magnificent example of the best craftsmanship and materials. It was custom designed by architect Winton Newhouse back in the early 19th century, but looks like it is brand new. All six bedrooms have large, walk-in closets which is something you just don't find in older homes. Four bedrooms, as well as the master bedroom, have adjoining baths and the powder room on the first floor is the biggest powder room I have ever seen. Have you seen the kitchen and rear yards, yet," he asked.

"Not yet," replied Stephanie, "we're heading that way now. I did notice a very large dark area on the oak flooring in the formal living room. Know what that is all about?"

I had seen the same stained flooring when we walked through, but thought how good an area rug would look there, and how well it would cover the darkened flooring. I think by the time we got to the kitchen, Stephanie was ready to have me write a check. Even more so after she saw the spectacular kitchen, eat-in area, and food pantry. That cinched the deal with her. Large, new six-burner gas stove with double ovens and a large, rectangular warming grill on the top made her day. While Stephanie didn't cook, she admitted to me one evening that her home had to have a bigger range than her sister, Andrea. Apparently Andrea was a gourmet cook of some repute, as well as trying to save the world. Stephanie would not have anything less, and this kitchen was certainly more!

"There's your boat house, lift, and dock," Stephanie told me as we strolled across the beautiful back patio and garden area. Looking toward the river, we saw a very large boat house, and a dock capable of handling a sixty-five foot yacht. The boat house had been designed and built to be a miniature of the mansion. Right down to the gables on the roof.

"Very nice" I said. "And the grounds are as spectacular as the house. Leaves very little to be desired. It's a good thing I'm not a do-it-yourself type of husband; I would be very happy with the lack of projects here."

"Do you even own a hammer?" Stephanie asked me.

That wasn't the point, as far as I was concerned. A simply gorgeous, move-in-ready, house without anything to fix, is a true jewel to me. Where do we sign?

"Howard, how is the wi-fi strength here? Is there anything we would be worried about? I ask because both Stephanie and I must have fast, reliable internet connections for both of our jobs. Me even more so now that my publisher has gone almost completely digital."

Howard must have anticipated my question because he had some charts showing where all internet suppliers' towers, and repeaters, were located. "With so many estate homes, almost all of whom are owned by wealthy business tycoons in this immediate area, all suppliers have targeted their best equipment, fastest connections, and widest bandwidth to this region of Connecticut. I don't think you will be disappointed at all."

We finished our tour looking at a gardener's shed and greenhouse on the North side of the property. As we strolled around the exterior of the house, I was picturing how my office could be set up for maximum efficiency. I could tell Stephanie was deep in thought, also. Probably decorating each and every room in her head. I asked Howard what the asking price was, and how long before they would be listing it for sale. He said it would go 'public' by the end of next week, and if we are interested we should make an offer today so we could go by the other realtor's office to close the deal. I was pretty certain of what Stephanie's decision would be, but I asked Howard how long he would be in this area.

"Several more hours probably," he replied. "I have to go down I-95 to Norwalk and make arrangements for my father. He is in a senior care facility that is closing Monday and I need to move him to another one. So I will be within a thirty to forty-five minute drive."

"Great," I said, "Let us get my car, have a bite of lunch and discuss this for a bit and I will give you a call. It seems too good to be true; especially at that price. I would not like to miss this opportunity."

Howard took Stephanie and I back to where I had parked my car in the lot at the diner, said his "good byes," and continued on westward down I-95 toward Norwalk. Meanwhile, Stephanie and I decided to 'live' a little and have lunch in a diner.

CHAPTER 5

There was a lot, I mean a lot, of discussion during our 'diner' dining. Talk about the menu, talk about the food, and lots of talking about the house. Stephanie asked our waitress where the locals went to do shopping. She asked about fine dining restaurants, which seemed to annoy the waitress. She asked about the local train station and how far it was from where we were seated.

Every question was followed by an answer that seemed to make the proposition that much more of a 'done deal.'

The waitress asked if we were moving into the area, to which Stephanie told her we had looked at a house that really peaked our interest. If we could get the right deal we definitely would be. That remark brought a huge smile to the waitress's face as she welcomed us home and asked if we would like more water.

After our lunch, we drove around town looking at different areas. We drove through downtown Westport, past an old maritime museum, and a lot of restaurants. Stephanie knew she would love Westport when she saw a Tiffany's store on Taylor Place, midway between a sushi place and a Starbucks'. We both decided that we needed to seal this deal and get back to wedding planning. Seems that there were only four more weeks until our wedding and we still had much to do.

I phoned Howard and told him we wanted to make an offer on the Victorian mansion. He had just finished moving the last of his Father's belongings into the new senior care facility, and agreed to meet us at the realtor's office. After many attempts at giving me directions, Howard asked where we were at. After finding signs with street names on them, Howard said he would come to us and we could follow him to the realtor.

It wasn't even an hour before Howard showed up and pulled along side of our car. He told me to follow him and he would drive slowly. I told him if we got separated for any reason, that I would call his cell phone. And with that he drove off.

The realtor's office was an unassuming, weathered building on the west side of Westport. Sandwiched between the Panera Bakery and Whole Foods Market on highway one, it looked like something from an old time movie, set in the great Canadian wilderness. Downstairs was his office, and upstairs his living quarters.

"David Jessup", Howard said, "this is the young couple I spoke to you about. They have seen the Victorian on Stony Point Road and are interested in making an offer. I think you'll find them good, kind people to work with." With that David Jessup and I shook hands and he showed the three of us to some old, cane-backed chairs placed directly in front of his desk. A desk cluttered with stacks and stacks of papers. In fact, the entire office area was cluttered with stacks of everything imaginable; old newspapers, old magazines, old everything just everywhere.

Stephanie dusted off her chair before sitting down and looking at the man behind the desk. David Jessup smiled at Stephanie and looked at me saying "so you have an interest in the Victorian, do you? Well I doubt seriously that you will ever see another house built that well with so many features and sculptured, manicured grounds. Nearly three acres of land, to boot."

"We're interested," I replied, "if the price and terms are good. Otherwise, there are a lot of nice homes available. We know, we have looked at a lot them."

"How many have been as nice as Stony Point, and how many have you made an offer on? He asked as I shifted in my chair listening to the creaking sounds it made. David Jessup went on to try to tell us about all the features the house had, but was interrupted by Stephanie.

"Mr. Jessup, we are very busy people. We have appointments in the city and do not have time to chit-chat. We have toured the house, we have seen the dock, boat house, and everything else. Let's get down to talking dollars or we'll have Howard show us more houses." Now there was the Walker family bluntness I was familiar with as Stephanie smiled back at

David and turned to throw me a quick wink.

The negotiations went back and forth for twenty minutes when finally David Jessup stood up from his chair and said "We have a deal." He walked over to his front office window and stared outside for several seconds. "I'll draw up the preliminary paperwork and get escrow going tomorrow. Can you give me a check of some amount to get escrow going?"

I was greatly surprised at this point because we had not even come up to half of what we were prepared to offer. Something was wrong as we were buying a ten million dollar house for a fraction over one million. I asked David Jessup if he had to call someone, like the seller, to get their approval for the agreed-upon price. He informed us that he had full power-of-attorney from the seller and could make any, and all decisions regarding the property.

"I, er, we can give a personal check now, or we can get a bank draft first thing Monday morning."

"Personal check will be acceptable. How much?" asked David.

Stephanie took her checkbook out of her purse and began to write a check. "How much is needed to begin escrow, Mr. Jessup? I can write up to fifty thousand dollars, but prefer not to, at this time."

David Jessup told Stephanie to make the check payable to him, note 'escrow' in the memo, and that five thousand would be fine. He then went to an old, somewhat unstable file cabinet and removed an old book of paper receipts. Complete with carbon paper. Was this a museum?

It took another hour to finalize the little bit of paperwork with David Jessup, get copies of everything and bid farewell to both David, and Howard Wilkins. We still had several hours drive to get back to the city and the day was soon to fade into night.

Howard walked out with us and thanked us for using him to find a house. We, in turn, thanked him for his knowledge of the area, and especially for finding this particular house. Howard said that David Jessup does not like much of what a realtor has to do to sell properties. He especially does not like the advertising, and promoting, aspects of home selling. He doesn't like taking multiple couples for tours of properties for sale. Nor does he like having to hold open houses, at all. We did him a huge favor by eliminating all those parts of selling this house.

We told Howard we were glad to have helped them both but we had to get going.

Howard thanked us again, and bid us safe travelling. He said he was available at any time if we had questions, or needed anything. With that we walked around the corner of the old building to my car.

Both Stephanie and I noticed the pungent odor the minute we exited the realty office. Something between sewer gas and old rotting flesh, or meat. Not bad enough to choke either of us up, but very noticeable and annoying.

Before I pulled the car onto the street, both Stephanie and I 'high-fived' each other, laughed and admitted that we could not believe our luck. "Be careful" said Stephanie, "the car could be bugged and David Jessup might hear us and want to cancel the deal."

I said that I doubted it, gunned the engine as we got onto I-95 south and we were New York City bound. House purchased, we were now anxious to let all our friends and family celebrate with us.

CHAPTER 6

The wedding went well. I guess that's a man's viewpoint, because according to the females involved, it was 'fabulous', 'glamorous', 'absolutely incredible', and 'simply the best wedding anywhere, anytime'. All I know is that everything went off without problem one. The bride was absolutely stunning in her off-white dress, and the groom was his usual handsome self. The priest kept everyone in stitches with his humorous comments. Stephanie's brother, and mine, did their readings without stumbling on any names or biblical terms. The organist and the choir were completely in tune with each other, and it was all over with within the three week time frame. Or so it seemed. After all, Stephanie had had lots of practice already with her previous weddings.

With both of us having to box up our respective apartments, getting every possession ready for the movers, as well as work and other commitments, we were not able to slip away on a honeymoon. We promised each other that would be changed as quickly as was possible. We hadn't decided where, or when, just that we would definitely do it.

In between court sessions Stephanie had found an interior decorator to help her with the decorating of her new mansion. Me? I just wanted to get my office set up right away and get busy with book eleven. Sorrabon Publishing was really on my case to get them the draft of book eleven, even though our agreement said the next book would not be required for another year, or more. Maybe they thought that me being married now, I would have too many distractions and not get eleven done on time. Who knows? I simply did not like disorder, and not having my home office done was certainly disorder to me.

Stephanie had decided to sub-let her apartment to a sorority sister who had just taken an accounting job close by. This worked out well for both women as Stephanie would have an "emergency" bed available if she ever got caught in the city late at night or needed to rise and appear early some morning. Her sorority sister liked the apartment so much that she gave us six months' rent money in advance. They also worked out some sort of code in case the other woman had a 'friend' stay over. Everything seemed to be falling into place for both apartments. Mine I let go back to the owner for renting out, again. I didn't feel the need to try to sublet to anyone, although a young fellow at Ben Haberman's office did ask about it several times. "Too much money for him," I thought. Much, too much.

Stephanie was in the height of her glory with decorating and re-arranging things. She had given top priority to my home office, so I was extremely happy with whatever was going on outside my closed office doors. I had another brilliant concept for book eleven, so I consumed every day with expanding this brilliant concept and putting it into book form. I felt that as long as I knew where my dresser was at in the master bedroom, where some food was at in the kitchen, and where my toiletries were at in our master bath, I was a happy man. Happy men sometimes do great work. That was the case with me, as my book eleven concept just kept getting better and better. "This one's bound to be the best novel yet." I told myself as I toiled day after day.

It was a couple days later that I heard the crash sound. Something fell; something heavy and noisy. I figured the interior decorator or one of her workers had dropped something. I decided to get myself a snack and check to make sure that whomever dropped whatever, that no one was hurt. I walked out of my office into an absolutely empty, quiet house. No decorator, no workers, no Stephanie. It was then I remembered that Stephanie had a partners meeting this morning so she would be gone. The decorator? Who dropped what to make that loud crashing sound?

I walked around the entire first floor before going up the steps to the second. There was not a sign of anything out of place. The third floor the same way. Everything perfect and quiet. Maybe I simply imagined it; imagined a loud crashing sound from a heavy object.

Yep. I imagined it. However, I was not imagining that horrible pungent odor. Where was that coming from? First the crashing sound and now a dead-meat-kind of odor. Bad enough odor that all thoughts of a snack disappeared the moment I walked into the kitchen. Must be something in the refrigerator, I thought, but was unable to find anything spoiled, nothing rotting in there. Check the ovens, maybe Stephanie left some meat in one of them from a few days ago. Empty and empty. Both ovens sparkling clean. I'd better check the food pantry.

Everywhere I looked there was not a single trace of any rotting, or spoiled anything. Nothing could be pointed to as to be the source of an ever-increasing bad, bad odor. What was causing this? I asked myself. Every cabinet, every drawer was just as Stephanie had set them up to be. Nothing. Then I thought about going down into the basement and checking to see if we may have some sort of sewer problem. At times the odor switched between rotting meat and a sewer smell.

But going down into the basement would rank as one of my least favorite things to do. Since I was a child, I've had a slight fear of darkness. Combine that fear with the ever-increasing odor which could be coming from the basement, combined with spiders and other creepy-crawlers, and I really had to have a long talk with myself.

Talk over, I inched my way down the newly widened, and remodeled stairs. Stephanie had many more lights installed down the steps and throughout the basement, also. Maybe she had some fear of darkness, also? Anyway, the lighted basement did not show any signs of sewer problems, and, in fact, the pungent odor was not detectable at all. Nothing other than the aroma of old cardboard boxes, and moisture was noticeable. Didn't even see any spiders while I looked around.

Then I heard it again. The loud crash of some heavy object as it hit the floor upstairs. No rolling around, no other sound; just the crash on the floor. Just as I looked upward toward the joists above me in the basement, the lights went out.

Complete darkness sent a cold chill right up my spine settling at the back of my skull. I had no reckoning skills to know where I could move to, or precisely where I was standing. In-body GPS was non-existent with this guy. Darkness so black, so dark that all senses of mine were lost.

It only took seconds before the panic level starting rising within me. Darkness so intense that I could feel it on my cheeks; feel it on my eyelids. It stroked my earlobes and it stroked my temple. It seemed to touch me everywhere. It touched me and choked me as I breathed it in. It was paralyzing me, making it impossible to move, even if I had known what direction to go. Darkness that I could hear breathing. Long, slow, deep breaths that made my fears even more intense. Darkness that almost seemed to be alive with an ability to suck life out of me. I felt I had to move; to go somewhere, but I was not able to. The darkness had captured me and was holding me captive. I listened to the intense silence and hoped that something would give me a clue as to which direction to turn. The darkness caressed me. Caressed me as if it was making love to me, but instead it was holding me captive. Captive with fear that was mounting more, and more. The darkness was winning, I thought. Winning the battle between my fears and its' ability to end my life. "Damn you, darkness", I screamed to no one. "Damn you," I whimpered to myself.

Suddenly there was blinding light burning my eyes. Light that created red and orange circles in my vision. Light that hurt. "Why don't you turn the lights on," asked Stephanie. "I had the contractor install all these new lights down here and you're not using them. Besides I thought you were afraid of the dark. Yet, here you are playing in it."

"Hardly call what I've gone through 'playing'," I replied, "I came down here to investigate where a loud crash sound may have come from, and while I was looking around, the lights went out. I didn't turn them off, they just went out by themselves. And, no, I'm not over my dislike of the dark. Still unnerves me."

"Sorry, I was just very surprised that you were down here and the lights were not turned on. I got home, saw you were not in your office working, and heard you yell when I walked into the kitchen." Stephanie came down several steps and bent over to look around the basement. "What was this 'sound' that you heard? Did you find what caused it?"

"I don't know what caused the crashing sound. I can't find anything that could have caused it, but it's not the first time that I've heard it. It has happened before. Still, no visible cause. Then the damn lights went out. I'm beginning to wonder about this place." I made a move to start up the stairs, but Stephanie was standing there, not moving and looking at me with a puzzled look on her face.

"Wonder about this place?", asked Stephanie. "What do you mean by that?"

I wondered how to go about explaining my feelings, my suspicions to Stephanie without sounding foolish. Do I simply talk about the crashing sounds that happen sometimes? Do I bring up the pungent, horrible smells that seem to emanate from everywhere, and nowhere? How about the day that the water stopped running while I was taking my shower? Doors being stuck closed, and not being able to open them. And now, the basement lights going out without anyone being around to flip a switch. How do I explain my feelings about all these occurrences? "It's just that...well, there are more and more strange things happening that seem to happen without any visible cause. Like the basement lights going out. Like the repeated crashing sounds that never show any reason for it happening. Like last week when you were in the city for an early morning meeting and I was getting ready in the bathroom. I started the shower, adjusted the water temperature, got in and got lathered up and without warning the water shut off. Not really shutting off, as such. The water just stopped flowing?"

I could see the look of disbelief on Stephanie's face, and wondered if I had said too much. I had no explanation for any of these 'events', so discussing them was going to be pointless. Still, Stephanie turned to start up the steps saying, "why don't we have a cup of tea and talk about this. Apparently, more is happening that I was aware of. IF, it actually happened." Stephanie had reached the kitchen and was grabbing her antique tea kettle from the stove top to fill it with water. I had remained motionless unsure if I was going to exit the basement, or not. I wanted to know much more about what happened, but reliving the paralyzing fears that I had gone through, made me unsure about moving. I stood there looking around and wondering about events when I heard Stephanie yell down to me that the "tea is ready." I turned and climbed up the stairs to the lighted doorway at the top. As I reached for the switch to turn off the basement lights, they suddenly went off! By themselves! Without me touching the switch! The basement was encased in utter, complete darkness! Again.

The tea was hot and delicious. Explaining the strange events which have occurred in this house, was not as delicious. Stephanie always saw the root cause of any occurrence, but could not see anything logical in what I was talking about. She asked me, point blank, "why don't any of these 'things' happen when I'm around? They only happen to you when you are by yourself. I can't say that I have ever witnessed even one of your 'events'. Not one." She continued sipping her tea without taking her eyes off me.

"I can't explain, nor answer that. I just assumed that you had experienced some of them yourself. I never thought about it happening only when I was alone in the house. Is there a chance that you don't believe me that these things are happening when I say they are?" I took another drink of my tea, but wished that it was something much stronger. Perhaps stronger, and alcoholic.

Stephanie never took her eyes off me. After what seemed like many minutes she said, "It's not that I do, or don't believe you, I'm sure that you believe what you're saying is real. It's just that in the real world I deal in, I deal with facts. What you're relating to me does not seem factual. It does not seem real." Stephanie took our tea cups and put them into the dishwasher. She asked me if I was hungry, or not, as she opened the refrigerator door to examine its' contents. She named off several choices that she saw without really sounding certain about any one of them.

"Actually, I was coming downstairs to get a snack, and, to investigate the crashing sound I heard earlier. Part of my investigating was to check out the basement. I regret that. Darkness is not my friend!" I answered as I walked toward the opened refrigerator door, and Stephanie. After looking at the contents, I suggested that a sandwich might be a good choice. That was the easy part: a sandwich. Now comes the hard part: what kind? Decisions, decisions. Will probably have whichever one Stephanie chooses.

"I think I'll have a 'TTL' on some of that fresh all-grain bread I bought at Panera Bakery," was Stephanie's decision. "The bread tasted really good when I sampled it, the other day."

"That sounds good to me," I replied, deciphering a 'TTL' as being a 'Turkey, Tomato and Lettuce' sandwich. I grabbed some things from the refrigerator as Stephanie went to get the bread, knives, and other items we need. Stephanie was good at fixing breakfast and most lunches, but did not possess her mother's, or sister's, cooking skills for dinners. She always admitted, when asked what her best dish is, that her best dish created, was a "snack." I always welcomed any long breakfasts or lunches that we had together, because they seemed to be few and far between. With me always being tied to my word processor, and Stephanie seemingly always either in partners meetings or in court, we both had a lot of solo meals. Dinners usually became something special for us.

"This bread reminds me that I'd like to go to church this Sunday," added Stephanie

"And that's because the bread is a cousin of the host we

receive during communion?" I quizzed. Seemed like a far, far stretch to me.

"Of course not, silly. It's because when I bought the bread, Susan, the owner of our Panera Bakery, mentioned to me that her granddaughter was being baptized this Sunday. I thought it would be a good time to show support to some neighbors, and to return to church." She said as she handed me a plate with my sandwich and some barbeque potato chips on it. I went looking for the jar of dill pickles I had bought while perusing the shelves at Whole Foods. Something tasty and soothing about a good dill pickle.

"You and your dills," Stephanie said as she sat at the counter portion of the kitchen island. "I love this house; love everything about it and just wish I could have less time in the city and more time here to really enjoy it. I'm concerned, though, that you may be working too hard on your novel. It may be starting to have an effect on you."

"You mean as in hearing things, or smelling things that no one else does?" I asked. I bristled at the thought that Stephanie might think that this was all my imagination. Not something I wanted to consider.

"Well, you know how over work, and stress had an effect on Jeff Thomas from CNN," she added. "He finally cracked that night from all that work. Right in the middle of the Democratic

Convention and they had to take him out of the arena in a jacket. Not a navy blue sports' jacket, either."

Our conversing was interrupted by the ringing of the phone. My reaction was rather jumpy and startled. Stephanie answered it on the third ring and told me that the caller wanted to speak to me. Was I in? was her question with her hand over the mouthpiece. When I asked who was calling she gave me a shrug of her shoulders. I thought for a few seconds before getting down off my barstool.

"Hello," I said putting the phone to my ear. "Hi, Guido. How are you doing?" Guido had been one of my groomsmen at our wedding but was not able to attend our housewarming party we had given after moving in. "I wondered if, maybe you had fallen off the edge of the earth. I have phoned but I keep getting a message saying your number was no longer in service. I didn't know where you had gone to, or if something might have happened to you."

Guido went on to tell me how he had taken a job which had him working overseas most of the time since our wedding. He was in Berlin and Frankfurt when we had the house warming celebration, so was not able to attend. He said he wanted to send postcards but did not have our new address with him. He finally got back to the states and found our address and new phone number. He talked on, and on about how much traveling he was doing with his new position for another eight to ten minutes, and then finally stopped.

"Any chance we could get together for dinner on Thursday? I'll be in Hartford and would love to see you and Stephanie," Guido asked. "There's a great chop place on 44th Street called the Capital Grille. Is Hartford too far to go for dinner?"

"Stephanie's in court Thursday afternoon and has to stay in the city for an early Friday partner's meeting. I'm available, and nothing in this state is too far. Especially for a friend," I replied.

We agreed on the place and time and said our 'goodbyes'. As I hung the phone up I couldn't help but wonder if there was another reason for Guido's sudden reappearance and phone call. Oh, well, I thought, it will be great to see him.

Stephanie went back to her previous conversation about stress and working too hard, to which I added, "Aren't you always the one who has the late client meetings, and the late-night into-the-early-morning stretches preparing briefs, and such? I'm pretty much on my own schedule most of the time. Occasionally a pending deadline creeps up on me and surprises me. But there is much less stress and 'over work' for me than there is for you."

With that statement I got a tilt of her head, a slow-to-form smile, and her decision to go upstairs and clean up. Discussion over.

I looked at the clock and decided that it was time for a cup of coffee. The new, single-cup-from-one-tiny-pod method of making coffee was a tremendous boon to mankind. Keurig should own the world, or at least control all of the civilized parts of it. To be able to make only one cup of coffee, or tea, late in the afternoon, or late at night when I was being really creative with writing, was phenomenal. After the computer and the iPhone, or iPhone and the computer, the Keurig method of creating hot drinks was the best invention ever. I would enjoy my single cup of 'French Dark Roast' coffee in my office and read today's emails, most of which were advertisements.

The afternoon passed in a very lazy sort of way as I pounded the keys of my computer doing some rewrites to chapters and a couple characters that I was not pleased with. I knew that I was expected to produce, as Ben Haberman would term it, a 'Platinum' level novel with every effort. Although my contact with Ben decreased more and more as time passed. Seems he was always off to one of the firms' other subsidiaries to straighten something out, or to terminate someone. Ben would become president of Sorrabon Corporation in three months when their current president stepped down.

Yes, Sorrabon Publishing had acquired several other publishing firms, along with two upstate radio stations and a total of three television stations. They sold off several book stores which had been acquired, along with two of the publishing companies, and they were now requiring all of Sorrabon's novels to be published in digital format. Somewhere along the acquisition road, Sorrabon bought two of the country's largest tech firms for designing and building their websites and writing code for their various companies. They were definitely diversifying and Ben Haberman would soon be at the top of all their totem poles.

I worked at my rewrites until my mind was blank and empty of ideas. I knew I was rewriting a winner and wanted to keep going, but I learned many years ago when the mind begins to quit providing ideas, it's time for the rest of the body to quit.

Even another cup of Keurig dark roast would not correct this.

CHAPTER 7

The drive up I-95 to I-91 north to Hartford was an easy drive except for the occasional erratic driver. With good weather and beautiful landscapes all around, the drive passed quicker than the two hours I had planned for it. I found my way to downtown Hartford and onto Columbus Boulevard. Although Hartford is the Capital of Connecticut, its' population is only about one-hundred-fifty-thousand people. It has been the scene of much of America's history, but it's downtown area is a plethora of one-way streets. Right now I was not concerned with any of that past history, only with navigating Hartford's roadways. I finally found my way onto Arch Street and around to Front Street. As I pulled up to the Capital Grille two valets came to my car to assist me.

"Welcome to the Capital Grille, Sir,' said the valet opening my door for me. "We'll park your car in a secure area and retrieve it when you have finished. Here is your ticket, Sir."

I thanked him, took my ticket and grabbed my topcoat from the passenger seat. As I walked to the entrance it occurred to me that I had never asked Guido about whether he, or I, should make a reservation. Now comes to mind the question: "Do we even have a dinner reservation, or will we be eating across Columbus Boulevard at the Subway sandwich shop?" As I went through the front door I saw Guido sitting on a stool at the bar. He waved as soon as he saw me and motioned for the bartender.

"Guido, how are you?" I asked, seating myself on the barstool next to him. "I hope that you had the presence of mind to make a reservation for tonight." He assured me that he had and that we still had plenty of time for a drink or two.

"Really appreciate you meeting me here for dinner. Have a lot of catching up to do. How was your drive up here?" Guido seemed to be a bit nervous as he rolled off one question after another. "How is Stephanie doing?" he asked, as I picked up my martini and took a sip. The martini was not bad, but not as good as in the city, I thought. It was then that I noticed that Guido had added several pounds around the waist. His dark grey suit, while well tailored, did not begin to hide the extra weight he carried.

"Stephanie is fine, and sorry she could not be here tonight to see you. She had an important trial due to finish up this afternoon and has to attend an early morning meeting of the firms' partners. She loves the new house in Westport, and has taken it on as her latest pet project." I sipped my drink and made a mental note to get into the city and have a drink from my favorite bartender. "So, tell me about this new job that has you traveling all the time. Lots of foreign travel? Or, mostly throughout the states?"

"The new job? Oh, it's okay. Lots of traveling around the

country and lots of foreign travel, too. It is a VP of Finance position and involves auditing various subsidiaries for a British corporation. I'm not really that fond of the job, but the paydays and the perks are great!" Guido was always the type of person to jump from job to job to job when the 'itch' got him. As an accounting major in school, he had held jobs ranging from bookkeeping, to sales manager, to salesman, and as president of a nineteen person hardware company. He always seemed destined to travel a great deal with whatever position he held. We were fairly good friends through school but drifted away from each other from time to time as I went through my first marriage's daily wars and conflicts. Guido had his own problems, also, with alcohol, pregnant girlfriends and just one thing after another. His mother contacted me at one point to see if I could, or would, talk to him, but I could not locate him.

We talked about old times, current events, old friends that neither one of us had seen in a while, and were about to get into discussing politics when we were told our table was ready. We finished the last drops of our drinks and followed the young man to our table.

Dinner was superb. One of the better cuts of meat I have had and cooked to perfection. Everything about the evening was great except for Guido being so jumpy, and on edge. As he ate his meal he constantly looked around as if he was expecting someone to show up. He reacted nervously to anyone walking past, and to any sound made. We ordered an after-dinner sherry and cup of tea to give us more time to talk. Guido never seemed to relax completely.

"What happened to your political career?", I asked. "I heard that after being mayor of Hartford, that you were on the short list for becoming governor of the state."

Guido looked around the dining room saying, "I found after a little more than a year that I didn't like politics. Either as mayor of a small city, nor would I like it more as state governor. I just couldn't get into the 'political mold' with what was being required of me. Fortunately, the mayor's position was an appointment with only twenty-two months of my predecessor's term having to be served. Then I was supposed to be a 'shoe-in' for re-election for two four-year-terms of my own before moving on to state office. I had to end it; end it quickly. I decided not to run for re-election and made a whole hell of a lot of people mad. Really mad."

I let that information settle in and processed it while I watched Guido continue to look around. I didn't care for the type of tea that they brought, but figured that I would drink it anyway. Needed something to offset the alcohol that I had consumed.

"I've never been one to advocate staying with a job that you just didn't like," I said. "I did that for too long at Sterling

Corporation when I took their sales manager position and found that I couldn't manage people according to their policies. They wanted Attila the Hun management styles and I could not play that game." I checked my watch to see how late it was getting to be and continued, "It kept getting harder and harder every day I was there. I brought my anger and frustration home with me, and eventually it helped to cost me my marriage."

My conversation, and thoughts, were interrupted at that moment by a well dressed elderly woman who had stopped next to our table.

"Get out of here, you son-of-a-bitch! Get out! Get away from decent people! Leave!." she screamed at Guido. She raised her right arm, purse and all, as if she was going to strike a blow, but the man standing next to her gently grab her arm and told her that they had to leave. "You deserve to be in hell!" she told Guido before being led down the aisle and out of the restaurant.

I could feel the intense stares coming from the other diners sitting all around us. Almost as if they were staring right through both of us. Guido, because the lady's tyrant was directed right at him, and me because I was seated at the same table with him.

"Well, that certainly was weird," I said to Guido. "What do you suppose her problem is? Do you know her?" I watched

Guido's expression change from surprised nervousness to more anger-induced nervousness.

"I have no fu…" Guido said, ending abruptly. "I have no idea. Never saw her before; don't know what she was angry about. Don't know why…". Guido paused, took a deep breath and looked directly into my eyes. "Obviously a real psycho case." Looking at his watch he added, "I had no idea it was this late, and I have a flight to catch in the morning. I really want to thank you for meeting with me tonight and would like to ask a favor of you. Can we meet, again, after I get back from this trip? I really need to talk to you about some things, but I'm off to Singapore and Myanmar. Can we do that, please?" Guido seemed almost to be begging me to meet again, and, of course, I could not say no. I asked if it was something that we could discuss now, offering to get a room in town for the night. Guido got up from his chair after paying the check and said he needed much more time than we had available tonight. Important things take longer than simply 'catching up' on our lives, and days out of touch. Much longer because there will be questions to be answered.

Now Guido was really peaking my curiosity.

Outside the restaurant, we shook hands and I thanked Guido for dinner and assured him that I would definitely make time available when he returned. Simply give me a call. I turned to hand the ticket for my car to the valet, and turned back to say more to Guido. He was gone! In less than ten or fifteen seconds he had completely vanished. It was as if he had been picked up by an invisible helicopter, hovering above us, and taken off into the low clouds and fog. Well, I will wait for his phone call.

The drive home seemed a lot longer than the drive to Hartford had been. Maybe it was the martinis, or maybe it was the strange lady and her angry burst of hatred. Anyway, the traffic was light and I had a good, old-time rock and roll, music station on my 'XM' radio.

CHAPTER 8

The angry woman from the night before, and her swearing at Guido still bothered me the following day when my thoughts were interrupted by the phone ringing.

"Hello", I said as I answered it. "Yes, this is he." The female voice on the other end sounded very soft but nice as she introduced herself and apologized for calling so early. "It's not really that early, but go ahead. What can I help you with?" She was calling to see if we could set up a time to meet. Her name was Sarah Douglas, and she is now my new publishing agent at Sorrabon. This caught me by surprise, and, of course, my question to her was what had happened to Ben Haberman.

"Mr Haberman has assumed his new position as the President of Sorrabon Corporation as of yesterday, and all of his previous 'preferred clients' have been transferred to me." Sarah Douglas said. "You are one of our very top clients, and I would like to get to know you better on a face-to-face basis. I was even reluctant to phone you with this request, having never met before."

Actually, Ms. Douglas and I had met before, but she did not recall the meeting. We met a little over a year earlier at a corporate function and were introduced to each other by Ben Haberman. I obviously made a good, lasting impression on Ms. Douglas.

"When did you have in mind?" I asked her.

"Today would be perfect if that is possible. After that, I would need to find an opening in both of our calendars. What are your thoughts?" she asked.

"I can catch a mid-morning train and be in the city shortly after lunch. What does your afternoon schedule look like?" I always took the train into the city when I made that trip. No one in their right mind ever, ever drove in New York City. Driving in the city was reserved for taxi drivers, and those bent on suicide by car crash.

"Two this afternoon will be good." Ms. Douglas added, as if there was only that time available. "Two o'clock in my office will do."

"And, where is your office? What floor?" I asked.

"The offices that Ben used to occupy are now MY offices. Those people work for me." She said with a tone of pure control over her 'domain'.

I told Ms. Douglas that I would see her at two in her offices and asked if I needed to bring anything with me. Like the latest rewrite of the next book? She said no and added that she did not like people who were late for appointments. With that admonishment ringing in my ears, I told her I looked forward to meeting her and would see her at two o'clock.

Now, it was time to get moving, get ready, and catch the train from Westport to the city. I sent Stephanie a text message, knowing that she was in the partners' meeting, that I had a two o'clock meeting at Sorrabon's offices with my NEW agent. I didn't really expect an answer, I just wanted her to know so, if, she wanted to meet later for dinner, or something, we could. It startled me a few minutes later when the 'text' tone on my iPhone told me that Stephanie had responded. It read: "in meeting...sorry...but, WHAT?" I decided that explanations could take more time than Stephanie or I had right now. We would not handle this by texting.

The train station in Westport was small, but very nice. Compact and very convenient for parking, leaving a car there safely, and catching either a westbound train to the city, or an eastbound train to Boston.

I was early, the train was on time. Surprised? That portion of the stress was eliminated.

There are good days in the city, and there are GREAT days in the city. Today had to be a great day! Sunshine, relatively good air quality thanks to a gentle breeze, relatively good traffic conditions, and a surprisingly small number of tourists milling about. City life on a day like today is what it's all about.

The taxi ride from the train station to 1735 44th street was comfortable and enjoyable. The driver conversed the right amount as I sat back and enjoyed seeing all the old familiar sights again. Seemed as though it had been years, and years since I left living in the city for the good life of rural Connecticut. Westport is my home town now, but New York City will always be my real home.

Getting into 1735 44th had not gotten any easier since my departure. In fact, the security has had several additional steps added to it which makes entry even more difficult. Seemed to me as though some sort of 'express lane' would make Sorrabon's "...very top clients" entry a much easier ordeal. Well, what do I know? On to the elevator's nice female voice.

"Good morning, sir, going up to Ms. Douglas's offices?" the female voice asked. After answering that I was indeed going up to see Sarah Douglas, I waited for the elevator to open, but it didn't. Seems that Ms. Douglas has already had one of the three elevators converted over to her very own private elevator and I needed to move two elevators to my left in order to use it.

On board the correct elevator, I noticed how nice, and elegant, it was. Newly redecorated, it showed signs of expense and craftsmanship. Inlaid walnut pieces in a strange design that reminded me of something I saw when researching Egyptian history. It had this same design repeated on every wall and the ceiling of the elevator. Someone really liked that pattern. I imagined that this new elevator décor might not be the only change I would find at Sorrabon.

The elevator door opened and there stood a tall, really good looking young man of about thirty years of age. Strikingly handsome, he looked as thought he had stepped right off the cover of 'Gents' magazine.

"Good morning, Sir, I am Bruce, Ms. Douglas's assistant. I will show you to her offices if you will follow me." And with that he did a somewhat military turn to his left and started down the hallway. Another change, I thought, as we went the opposite direction from where Ben's office used to be. At least the hallway had not changed...yet. As we got to the end, Bruce opened a door for me and a flood of noise came rumbling out from within. I stepped through the doorway to see about thirty-five, maybe forty, people racing about doing their things. No one was talking, the noise came from the 'piped in' music playing from everywhere. Bruce showed me to a large conference room and asked me if I preferred cold water, or fruit juice to quench my thirst.

I told him that water would be fine and he did his military style about-face and left.

The conference room was nicely furnished, though I felt Stephanie's decorator could have done a much better job for Sorrabon. But it was not my place to judge, or compare. The table was about twelve feet long and was flanked by rather simple padded seat and seatback chairs which could accommodate about fourteen people. There were three portraits hung on the walls, but only one did I recognize, and that was a very literal interpretation of a younger Ben Haberman. The others I did not know but suspected that the one at the far end of the conference room could be Sarah Douglas. Thinking about Stephanie I was reminded that I had not texted her that I had gotten to the city okay and should do so right away.

As Bruce returned with my glass of cold water, he noticed my iPhone in my hand. Sitting the glass down on a coaster on the table, he said "Sir, the phone will not work in this building. You cannot transmit or receive anything. We have special, multi-frequency radio waves that cancel any and all available frequencies for phones and all electronic equipment. The only things that go out, or come in, are transmissions done through our super-secure network. Very sorry, sir, but that is the way it is." And with that Bruce smiled and turned to leave the room.

"Thank you, Bruce. Who are these portraits of? I believe that one might be a very young Ben Haberman, but the other I do not know." I had stopped Bruce mid-step with my question about the portraits.

Turning back to me with a military style about face move, he smiled and sighed ever so slightly. He looked at the portrait on the far wall saying, "that, sir, is Charlston Dumenai, the founder of Sorrabon Company in Great Britain. That other gentleman is Mr. Ben Haberman, the current president of

Sorrabon Corporation, and it was just painted about a month ago. The third painting is, of course, Ms. Sarah Douglas, my boss and current president of Sorrabon Publishing. Her painting was just completed and hung here two days ago." With that Bruce did another military style about face and left me alone in the conference room. I put my iPhone back into my inner coat pocket and wondered how many more changes awaited my discovery. Wondered what happened to the old, magical glass walls that surrounded Ben's old office. Ben used to love flipping the hidden switch and turning the clear glass walls to very opaque glass walls. Another surprise for me; another hint of the past that was gone.

"Sorry to keep you waiting, but it is NOW exactly two, and I believe our meeting was scheduled to begin at two. Please, have a seat and let's get to know each other." All this was being said by a tall, very attractive, and very muscular, red-haired woman of, maybe, mid-thirties. She walked over to the only executive styled chair and sat down. She motioned me to have a seat and leaned back a bit.

"Let me repeat something I said on the phone earlier, and that is that Sorrabon truly cherishes its' "very top clients." You are definitely one of those people. However, we have some items we need to discuss in order to keep you in that exalted position." Sarah continued, "We need to rewrite our agreement with you."

I now felt like the number one pin on the lane at the bowling alley, and someone had just rolled a strike. "Excuse me?", I answered, "Rewrite what?" I studied Sarah's never-changing-facial-expression, and could not tell a thing about her, or what she had just said. "I believe that I have a contract with Sorrabon that I have complied with in delivering novels of top quality. Novels, I might add, that have sold millions of copies. Novels that have been published in thirteen different languages around the world. Novels that have made a ton, or more, of money for Sorrabon Publishing." I could feel my temperature and my BP rising, and knew that my face was turning more red as I spoke.

"Much of what you say is true, but don't forget that Sorrabon has paid YOU a ton, or more, of money while we assumed all the costs and risks of everything you threw together. You're being very one-sided about this and I, for one, would appreciate you looking at the whole picture. You're one of many writers whom we publish; Only one. Most of the others have already agreed to the new contracts and moved on with creating. We let you ride your gravy train for a lot longer!" Sarah had adjusted her seated position to a more upright position and had folded both hands across each other in front of her on the conference table. She stared directly at me without blinking or moving.

"I think that this is a subject that needs to be discussed

while my attorney is present. Is that where we are at, at this point?" I asked her and wished that I could text Stephanie right now.

"If that's the way you wish to handle this, then we need to end now and have your lawyer contact our legal department. Let me tell you a secret, though, our legal department has been to court twenty-seven times in the last year and has not lost a single case. Not one! So we can handle this on a friendly, personal, way, or another way. Your choice." With that Ms. Sarah Douglas stood up from her chair while continuing to stare directly at me.

"Sarah", I started to say, but was quickly corrected to 'Ms. Douglas'. "Sarah, you have already made the choice by the way you have handled this meeting, and by what you have said. You leave my current novel, which may just be my very best ever, in jeopardy and certainly all future novels in jeopardy." I tried to not get madder by the minute, but it was becoming more and more difficult to do.

"That's a pity that you are so self-centered that you will not, for one minute, take the high road and see the total picture here. Your contract expires the end of next month. You have a novel due ten days before the contract expires. You have a big, beautiful mansion that you need to pay for, and all you are concerned about is the old way that things were. Well, mister, times have changed. The publishing business has changed. Life has changed, and will be changing even more. You had better get on the new 'bandwagon' and realize this. If you walk out of here without signing a new contract, I can't guarantee that there will be another one. Ever." With that she looked at her watch. "It is now two-ten and I have another meeting in five minutes upstairs. Why don't I email you a copy of your agreement, you look it over, initial where indicated, sign it and return it to me within the next twenty-four hours? Will that be okay with you?" she asked as she turned without waiting for an answer and walked out of the conference room.

I sat there, by myself in the now empty conference room, and wondered what in the world had just happened. Did I just momentarily doze off and have some sort of dream? A nightmare, even? Did I go through some type of time warp and come out on the other side? What happened? Nothing made sense and yet the reality of me being here, in this conference room, touching this table, seeing the glass of cold water sitting in front of me with its' watery trails running down the outside of the clear glass, all this told me I had to be in a real world. A real world without any understanding of what I had just experienced.

Just then, Bruce entered and said, "Sir, your meeting has concluded, may I show you the way out?"

"The way out?" I thought. Just give me some time to get my bearings and then maybe I can stand up and walk out. Bruce asked me again, only this time I decided to leave on my own schedule.

Bruce stood close by like a good soldier would. "Sir, we need the conference room shortly for another meeting. I must ask you to leave. Please follow me to the elevator."

I gathered my thoughts as I rose from my chair, and asked Bruce how long he had worked for Ms. Sarah.

"She prefers Ms. Douglas, Sir, and it has been almost 11 years. Since I was in grad school. Why do you ask?"

"Curious, Bruce, just curious." We walked through the outer office where the same large group of employees were scurrying about like ants gathering food. Bruce stopped at the elevator button, pressed it, and bid me a good day.

"Hope you sign the new agreement, Sir, and return it within the twenty-four hours that Ms. Douglas has given you. She is an extremely punctual person. Right down to the minute."

With that Bruce walked back down the hallway and I entered the elevator to go down to the real world. Hopefully, the real world.

As I left the building and entered the masses of people rushing down 44th street, my iPhone started to sound off like crazy. Text messages, emails, everything that could be received via iPhone was suddenly being received. I watched as the number of each increased like they were 'tote boards' for a fund raiser. I saw three text messages from Stephanie telling me that she was out of her meeting, finishing some paperwork for a client to come in and sign, and asking me how things were going. The last text asked me about dinner at 'our' restaurant tonight.

I needed to read emails and answer Stephanie's text messages. I also needed to clear my head and to do some serious thinking. Serious thinking.

I hailed a taxi and told the driver to take me to the Central Park Zoo. I wasn't going to visit with the animals; I thought it would be a good spot to be dropped off and, when ready to leave Central Park, it would be a good spot to hail another taxi. I needed to walk through the park and think about the events and conversation with Ms. Sarah Douglas. I needed, as Stephanie would call it, "me time."

It was working. Walking through the park on a nice afternoon, watching people walk hand-in-hand, walking their dogs, and even one couple who had a cute little black miniature pig with a harness and leash. People who seemed relatively happy with the day; people who seemed to truly enjoy a day in the park's environment. People who did not have any dealings with Ms. Sarah. Well, the more I walked, and thought about things, the better I felt, and decided to go back and get a taxi to the restaurant. After a nice dinner with my lovely wife, and maybe a martini or two, decisions that have to be made, may just be much easier.

The taxi driver told me that we had to go a 'round-about' way to the address that I had given him due to many streets being closed on the east side of the park. The east side has a lot of foreign embassies and consulate buildings, and apparently some sort of threatening 'standoff' between a person with a complaint, and a bomb, and the NYPD was occurring in that area. So, to be safe, the NYPD had closed down much of the upper East Side area to traffic. Great! Another wacko gone wild, I thought.

The taxi driver finally found his way to the restaurant.

Walking inside the restaurant, I began to appreciate how comfortable some parts of our 'old' life can be. Familiar surroundings, a comfy environment, and a perfectly-made, dry martini. I checked my watch and saw that I had enough time before Stephanie arrived to enjoy a drink. I found an empty barstool positioned perfectly for a view of the entrance. To my surprise, the great bartender named Yuri was not behind the bar. An attractive, black hair, woman with bright green eyes was now handling customers requests. Apparently Yuri had left last week and gone back to his 'homeland', wherever that was. This young lady was now the 'keeper of the mixes.'

Oh, well. Another change in life to deal with. Just then I had a flashback to Sarah Douglas's statement about life changing. "...Life has changed, and will be changing even more." She had said earlier. God, I didn't want her to be right!

CHAPTER 9

Dinner with Stephanie was all about my afternoon meeting with Sarah Douglas. How she dressed. How she handled the meeting. What she threatened. Everything that I could remember was discussed in detail.

"Ten minutes?" Stephanie asked. "The meeting lasted only ten minutes? You've got to be kidding! Coffee breaks last longer than ten minutes!"

I told Stephanie about Bruce, Sarah's assistant, and how 'military' his movements seemed. How he came back into the conference room after Sarah left and just about escorted me out. How the really good martinis that Ben Haberman used to provide were now replaced by either 'cold water or fruit juice'. How lavish the new offices, and her personal elevator, were. Everything was different; not better, just different. I could envision Sorrabon needing a much higher percentage from authors just to pay off the improvements I saw.

"Have you looked at the new contract that they're offering?" asked Stephanie. "You said that Sarah was going to email it to you."

"No, not yet. I saw it on my iPhone, but it's too large a file to review on such a small screen. I figured I, or we, would look it over when we got home."

Stephanie finished her cup of tea saying, "Maybe we should leave now, catch the next train home, and look over Ms. Sarah's offer on your big screen desktop."

I agreed, paid the dinner check, and left with Stephanie to catch a taxi to Grand Central Terminal. Probably one of the busiest places on earth, regardless of the time of day or night.

We caught the Boston bound train and settled in for the ride back to Westport. Stephanie continued to have a few more questions regarding Sarah Douglas and our meeting, but we mostly just watched the passing scenery, and the people milling about on the train.

When we got home, we were very surprised that the front door would not open. "It's completely stuck closed," I told Stephanie. "I tried the key every which way; guess I need to get tough with it." Tough, to me, was to imagine that I was a pro football defenseman and put my shoulder to it with full force and skill.

"Damn, that hurts like hell" I said after giving all my energy into putting my shoulder to the door. All my energy, and now all I had was a very painful, aching right shoulder. The door still would not budge. "Let me go out to the gardening shed and get a hammer. That should do the trick." I told Stephanie, and asked her to 'guard' the door so that nothing happened to it. As I walked around the house to the gardening shed, I saw the lights in the house go on. "Oh, my God", I thought, "another freaky happening! The lights went on by themselves and I'm NOT by myself this time."

I ran back around to the front of the house to make sure that Stephanie was alright. There, to my great surprise, was the opened front door with Stephanie standing inside in the foyer. I stopped and stared in amazement. "What happened?" I asked. "How did you get inside?"

Stephanie was standing with her arms crossed in front of her, smiling. "I turned the handle. I turned the handle and the door simply opened. Just like it was supposed to. Don't understand what the problem was before, but all I did was to turn the handle."

I stood there in amazement looking into Stephanie's eyes. "Is this another weird happening with this house?" I asked.

"I don't know. Maybe you didn't turn the key all the way. I just don't know." Stephanie hung her coat in the closet and said, "Regardless, why don't you boot up your desktop and let's look at the email from Sarah Douglas. I'm more concerned about the contract and what they are trying to do to us." With that, Stephanie went upstairs to the bedroom to change, and I went into my office to start up my computer.

After forty-five minutes of reading, and re-reading, the email attachment, Stephanie sat back in her chair. "This is the worst attempt at 'involuntary servitude' I have ever seen. Not even in law school, did I see anything that was written this poorly. This would not hold up in any court in this country."

"Sarah boasted about the successes of Sorrabon's legal department this year saying that they had not lost a single case. Not one!" I told Stephanie as we flipped pages of our copies which I printed off. "I think she was trying to intimidate me, but she stated it like it was a well known fact."

"Don't care what she said, this is not a contract that conforms to state laws. I would love the opportunity to challenge her, or rather Sorrabon Publishing, on this matter." Her little bit of Irish was starting to surface in Stephanie's persona. She was a fighter; a tough one when challenged too far, or pushed into a corner.

"What are some of the other authors doing?", She asked. "Is every single writer signing this new contract without question? What about Dan Brown? What about Stephen King? What did John Bolsten do? Did they all sign?"

I, of course, had no idea what other authors had done. I was curious also, but had never talked to most of the other writers under contract with Sorrabon. "Stephen King has not been with Sorrabon for years, and I do not know about Dan or John Bolsten. I think I may have John's cell phone number somewhere, but I'm sure I don't have any info on Dan Brown."

Stephanie put her copy of the agreement down saying, "I vote we go to bed, get up early in the morning and start making phone calls. I can probably get my office to get contact information for Dan Brown. It would be good to have you make a list of every writer you can think of that is under contract to Sorrabon. But for today, I think we need to call it a day."

I agreed, and put my copy of the new agreement in the top middle drawer of my desk. Before I could start to shut my computer down, the house went dark. Dark as dark can be! Not a sign of light anywhere inside, yet the outside lights were all very visible and bright.

"This is strange," I told Stephanie. "Very strange. Why would we lose electricity now? Why are only the house lights out, and not other lights outdoors?"

"I don't know," answered Stephanie, "but I don't like it. How are you doing with all this? You're the one with the real dislike of the dark."

"I'm not moving; barely breathing while I wait for the electricity to come back on."

"Do you still have a flashlight in the bottom drawer of the desk?" asked Stephanie. "How about using it to see our way around. Providing the batteries are okay."

As I opened the bottom left hand drawer of my desk, a low

moaning sound started to be heard. A moan like from a large animal. Maybe a big, brown bear making a moaning sound as if in pain. Painful moaning that continued; continued and gradually got louder, and louder. "Am I the only one who hears that?" I asked Stephanie.

"No, I hear it, but what is it? Sounds like a dying elephant giving its' last mournful breath. I also smell that horrible odor. God, what is that?"

"I don't know," I answered, "but this is some of what has happened before. Not the moaning, but the odor, and the blackout are some of the things I have experienced. The things which I think you may have thought were from my imagination. I'm sorry they're happening again, but I'm glad you're here when they are happening."

Again the darkness was all encompassing, caressing my skin, and taking the breath right out of my lungs. Paralyzing, captivating, unrelenting blackness that now had us both.

I found the flashlight, but after many attempts to turn it on, I guessed that the batteries were dead. I held it in my hand and wondered what to do next.

The moaning got louder. The odor kept getting stronger and more fowl smelling. Then, as if things weren't bad enough, there was a tremendously loud, crashing sound. A sound so loud that both Stephanie and I jumped.

"What was THAT?" she asked. "What would make that loud a noise? What is going on?"

All questions for which I had no answer. No idea of what was causing any of this. Then suddenly everything stopped. Everything was back to how it had been earlier. No odor, no more moaning sound, the lights were back on and the flashlight had a strong, perfect beam of light. Stephanie and I sat looking blankly at each other. Nothing to say. No movement. Just looking deep into each others' eyes...and wondering.

"I'm unsure about whether to stay down here, or go upstairs to bed," Stephanie said. "I don't cherish the thought of sleeping in my recliner tonight, but what if something happens during the night. What if we are awakened by a repeat performance?"

"Both of our recliner chairs are very comfortable, but my vote is to go to bed. My experience with these 'events' is that they happen once. Then they stop for a long time before happening again. I think we would be safe in our bed." For the first time I saw a hint of fear in Stephanie's eyes. Something I had never seen in her before; not ever. Not in all the years we had dated, been engaged, or married. She always was a strong, Walker-family-strong, determined woman. Now her eyes, and whole body language said, "what is happening here and why?"

As we both climbed into our bed and said 'goodnight' to

each other, we agreed that a single lamp left on all night would not disturb either of us while sleeping.

If we slept.

CHAPTER 10

The morning brought lots and lots of sunshine, beautiful blue skies, and lots of phone calls. Stephanie on her cell phone, and me on the house phone. Calling her office to enlist help in getting names of all writers under contract with Sorrabon Publishing, and any and all other information regarding Sorrabon Publishing that could be harnessed. Watching Stephanie work was like watching a general preparing for battle. She gave orders, right and left, to people in her office; she gave orders to others whom I didn't even know existed. She had both a mental, as well as a written, list of things she wanted. Exhausting, but she did it all with perfection.

Me, on the other hand, had found Dan Browns' cell phone number and had called and left him a message. The message was about why I called, and to please return my call. Even though Dan Brown and I had never met, there is an unwritten agreement between all authors that we help each other, up to a point. My questions, and needs, did not approach that point.

After several hours of phoning, researching on the internet, and at least four or five Keurig brews of coffee, I sat back in my office chair. "Wow!", I thought. "Wow. Wow. Wow!" How did we compile such a big stack of papers, all related to notes, information printed off the internet, and copies of clippings from various newspapers? This was just my efforts. No telling how much Stephanie had in her office.

As I felt my stomach rumbling a little, I looked at the clock on the wall. Eleven-thirty. This meant that IF we were going to sign and return the new agreement, we had only two-and-one-half hours in which to do it. Minus ten minutes as a 'safety factor.' After all, as Bruce had told me, Ms. Douglas "is an extremely punctual person. Right down to the minute."

I walked over to Stephanie's office to see how she was coming with her work only to find her office empty. She was no where to be seen. Ah, I thought, she's in the kitchen fixing something to eat. Empty again. If she was not in her office and not in the kitchen, she must be in the bathroom. I would wait until she appeared.

As I walked through the kitchen to the back porch area I saw Stephanie walking back and forth while she talked on her cell phone. She had a very disturbed, deep frown, expression on her face and her body actions seemed to denote some displeasure with whomever she was talking with. I exited the back door and started to wave at her when she put her cell phone into the front pocket of her jeans.

"How are you doing?" I called out to her. "We only have a couple hours left in Sarah's deadline."

She walked toward me without saying anything until she was within a couple feet when she said, "Some good news, some not-as-good-news. Let's grab some quick lunch and go over what I have and what you have discovered. This thing is so much bigger than either one of us could have imagined. Much bigger!"

With that, we went back into the kitchen where a bowl of soup and a couple sandwich halves were prepared. It was now twenty past twelve.

Stephanie took some soup before saying, "We have a bigger situation here than we thought. And, I have a couple problems before we deal with Ms. Sarah and Sorrabon Publishing. Problem number one is that...well, remember the big, end-of-year, partner's meeting I attended a couple months ago? That was when we distributed year-end profits among the partners, and by a vote of the other partners, I received a special six-figure added bonus. They felt that I have brought so much new business into the firm that I was entitled to something extra. Well, I used that extra money to buy you the boat that you wanted. It was suppose to be a surprise for your birthday, but they have to deliver it today." She waited for the completely shocked look to fade from my face before continuing. "That's one of the reasons that I took my phone outside was to try to get that mess straightened out without you hearing me. They screwed up the delivery date and are delivering your birthday gift two months early! I didn't want that! I wanted you to come home on your birthday and there it set tied up to our dock ready for you. Maybe even a big red bow tied around the helm. But, it's being delivered today. Oh, well, the best laid plans, I guess."

I couldn't believe what I was hearing. "You bought me a what?" I asked Stephanie. "A boat? We can't afford a boat, yet."

"Well, actually, we can afford it….and did! I still had some money left over to furnish my office with those rather pricey antiques I saw in Hartford. Now we need to save a few pennies so we can sail off to Bermuda for an extended vacation."

"I don't believe what I'm hearing, but tell about the boat before I pass out. Is this that forty-six foot Hunter that I saw at the Marina? Or, the forty-two foot Catalina that we saw for sale by the diner?" I asked.

"Neither" answered Stephanie, "I got that forty-nine foot Gulfstar Classic MY with the NAIAD Stabilizers that the boat yard sales company had on display. The commandant of the yacht club helped me decide. He said that this was his purchase of choice, and he is very envious of you. He, also, is holding your 'pre-approved' application for membership in his hand. Whenever you're ready, just phone and give him the missing info."

"I don't know how to say 'thank you' to you. It's just too unbelievable to even process right now." I told Stephanie as I grabbed her and gave her a huge, big kiss and hug. "Thank you. Thank you very much." We stood looking into each other's eyes after the hugs when the moment was broken by a loud crashing sound.

"What the hell?" Stephanie asked. "What was that noise?"

Stepping away and looking around, I answered "that, my love, is the noise I hear quite frequently that I can never uncover the source of. I'm glad you finally heard it, too."

We started looking all around the first floor knowing that something had fallen there. The more we looked, the less certain we were that something would be found. Then it happened again! A second, loud crashing sound as if several big metal cabinets had fallen upstairs. We both raced up to the second floor and started to search. Several minutes later we joined each other at the top of the steps and simply looked at each other.

"Nothing" Stephanie said, "I wasn't able to find a single thing out of place. How about you?"

"Ditto" I said. "Not one thing out of place, and certainly nothing has fallen that I can see."

Literally, we were scratching our heads with confusion when we heard a knock on the front door. The knock, and yet another crashing sound sent us scurrying down the stairs. Stephanie said she would get the front door if I would look for what crashed. Off we went.

The crashing sound was just one more invisible item; a.k.a., nothing found. The knock on the front door was the delivery men from Maritime Yacht Sales delivering my boat. Now, I was told, once, that when you own a boat larger than thirty-five, or thirty-six feet, you own a ship! So, my yacht was actually a ship! Not boat! Nonetheless, they had 'Google'd' our house and saw we had a boat slip large enough to handle my new toy, so they sailed it down the Saugatuck River, and tied it up at our docking area. Now they had to finish taking all the weather-protective coverings off, finish cleaning up some dirt and dust inside, and get the delivery papers signed.

"We just do delivery, sir" the one fellow said. "Our office will contact you to set up an appointment for a master seaman from our company to come over and go over all the equipment with you. I would plan on an entire morning or afternoon for that since this is quite a 'state-of-the-art' item."

Stephanie and I walked out to the dock with the three delivery men to watch them finish their delivery functions. We looked at each other with pride and wonderment at such a beautiful piece of craftsmanship. Even without knowing much about this particular yacht, Stephanie was in awe.

"She's beautiful" Stephanie said standing in the sun looking at it. "Sleek and streamlined, and just beautiful."

"Yes she is", I added. "But how do we know it's a SHE? It

could be a he."

Stephanie looked at me and raised one eyebrow and said, "Anything that beautiful, that sleek has to be a she. Now, we'll have to decide on a name for her."

One fellow heard Stephanie's remark and told us that when we set up the appointment with the master seaman, give him the naming information and a sign painter will come over at the same time as the master seaman to paint the boat's name on it. We simply stood there watching the three men do their work while the sun baked our faces a little.

It was only about an hour and a half before they completed their tasks, and I signed the delivery paperwork. They drove off in an old panel truck that one of the men had driven over from the sales office. Their tasks completed, the 'ship' was now ours to enjoy. As soon as I get fully instructed on all the equipment inside it. Never a shortage of things to learn.

"Oh, NO!" Stephanie exclaimed. "We forgot about the deadline for the new contract and it's now three twenty!" She looked at me in disbelief. "We had better get our 'stuff' together and discuss this matter because we still have a decision to make. Deadline missed, or not."

"Let's go back to the house now and get moving on it" I said still looking at the beautiful Gulfstar Classic that was tied up to our dock and now needed a name. The yacht was locked and secure for the time being, so we headed back across the back yard for the house.

"Stephanie, earlier you said you had a couple of problems, and I assume that the extra-early delivery of the yacht was only one of them. What was the other problem?"

"We have a real mess with this Sorrabon thing. A real mess. It involves people that we could not ever imagine being involved; it involves companies that we would never imagine being involved. This whole thing goes so many different directions that it's worse than a spider web. It also involves this house!" Stephanie paused and took a deep breath. "It involves Guido."

"Guido?" I asked. "Guido and this house? How could this house be involved with Guido? Guido has nothing to do with this house. I don't understand."

Stephanie took her collection of papers, emails, and such and made herself another cup of tea. "We need to start at the beginning. We've missed Sarah Douglas's so-called deadline, so that concern is already off the table. Secondly, the contract she wants you to sign would be found to be unlawful in almost every state of this country. It is written so heavily in favor of Sorrabon that it is ridiculous. They would get eighty percent, or more, of the profits from the sale of every book they publish. Print, digital, or any form that may be used into the future. Any form. The authors are responsible for all expenses derived from negative sales, and negative sales are quite possible the way the marketing program is arranged. Even a well known, brilliant writer like you would not see any money until your books sell in excess of one-half million copies. Sell four-hundred-thousand-ninety copies and you will be paying all of Sorrabon's losses. Nice deal, huh?"

I was listening intently to everything Stephanie was telling me. "I still don't understand how Guido is involved, though. Has he ever owned this house?"

"No," Stephanie answered, "it doesn't involve ownership. Let me do this from the top. Remember some time ago when I told you that the names Guido and Kiefer just didn't go together? That I thought something was wrong with that name combo. Well, Guido's real name is Gilbert. Guido Kiefer is really Gilbert Keeper. Let me know when this begins to sound familiar. He is currently the vice president of finance for Sorrabon Corporation. He is responsible for all corporation functions involving finances around the world. Sorrabon has become one of the world's large conglomerates. My firm has not finished digging through everything, but so far they own more of New York City than Trump Enterprises. Office buildings, apartment buildings, condos, retail outlets, it is quite a long list. They appear to even own the two realtors that we were involved with in the purchase of this house. So, we have Ms. Sarah

Douglas involved now. Ms. Sarah came to the publishing entity from one of their California divisions where there is an investigation currently going on involving money laundering and drugs from Central and South America. She's not quite ready for sainthood. Some people, that my office talked to, refer to her as 'Sarah-the-Assassin' because of her propensity to fire people left and right. Now, follow me into the living room and help me pull back the rug."

We walked into the living room, rolled the area rug back, and exposed the big, dark stained area of flooring. We stood there staring at it without saying a thing. Finally, Stephanie handed me a copy of a newspaper article. It was old and somewhat difficult to read in some areas. The headline, though, was clearly readable, it read: ENTIRE FAMILY MURDERED. The newspaper was dated March 17, 19xx. The rest of the date was torn away and missing. Okay, I wondered, what is this about? As I continued reading, things began to make more sense. The story under the headline told about an entire family of husband, wife and their four children being murdered by someone with an axe. "A bloody, brutal attack in the Connecticut town of Westport. The entire Keeper family, except one boy who was away on a camping trip, were murdered in cold blood. Police investigators were not able to determine how much blood was spilled in these brutal attacks, as the family's home was literally an ocean of blood. One police officer said that in his thirty one years of police work, he had never seen this much spilled blood." The article went on to tell readers that the Keeper family owned the market in downtown Westport, as well as the hardware store, an auto repair shop, and many real estate parcels. They also had many holdings in Texas oil fields at a time when oil was just beginning to show its' true worth. Apparently their family home was set in the middle of one-hundred-seventy-four acres of land alongside the Saugatuck River and was the site of the murder. It went on to tell of the family's history, and the connection with both Boston families, and with Washington, D.C. government officials. Not much was said about the surviving family member until some closing paragraphs. "The lone surviving family member is nine-year-old Gilbert who does not yet know how lucky he is to have been away from home. Young Gilbert Keeper II, was away on a camping trip arranged by a local church official for a group of boys. No one knows if Gilbert has been told of the murder of all his family members."

"Wow," I thought. All of this happened right here in Westport, in this town, in this house.

I looked at the huge, dark stain on the living room floor, then I looked at Stephanie. "So that is what we're looking at?" I asked. "Do you think that this murder of the entire Keeper family happened right here in this living room?"

"I can't imagine that it happened anywhere else." She said. "One of our criminal investigators also found an article published years later that claimed that Gilbert Keeper II was arrested for the murder of his family. But before he could be tried, he vanished and was believed to be living somewhere in Europe. Your Guido is his son and was born in Switzerland. A country without deportation agreements at that time."

"This is a great deal to process quickly." I said to Stephanie, handing the article copy back to her. "If this murder happened here, what does that mean for us? I don't see how all of this ties into this house, Sarah Douglas, and everything. I think I need a drink. How about you?"

"I haven't said anything to you, but I've had some strange events happen in this house. Like the back door slamming shut and locking me out all by itself. The door to the garden shed would not open one day for almost two hours, then suddenly opened all by itself. Brand new flowers that I planted outside were dead the following day. I took them back to the nursery and a botanist told me they had been soaked in weed killer and I should treat living things better." Stephanie told me that she would love a drink and to make it a strong one. She continued, "One day when I went to get my car out of the garage, first the side door into the garage would not open. Then after trying to force it open, it opened, but my car would not start. Then after the car finally started running, the garage door closes. If the side garage door hadn't stayed open because of a stone jamming it open, I would have been asphyxiated by the car's engine fumes."

We sat down in the dining room with our martinis and just stared back into the living room with its' rolled-back rug and rearranged furniture. Rolled-back rug, rearranged furniture, and huge, dark, blood stain. What do we do now, I wondered to myself. Where do we go from here?

"What do we do about Sarah Douglas?" I asked Stephanie. "I have to complete my current novel and get it to them for distribution by next month. A couple weeks after that my contract expires and I will be without a publisher. Not a good way to create income."

"What about forming a new publishing company?" she asked. "I have some multi-media clients who have talked about getting into the publishing side of things. Maybe we can battle Sorrabon Publishing on their own playing field. Get back at them with their own tools. If that doesn't sound appetizing then we can look for another publisher. You're certainly a well known entity with a very marketable name, so I don't think another publisher would turn away from the opportunity."

Doing battle with Sorrabon gave me mixed feelings. On the one hand, I didn't want to make life more difficult for Ben Haberman. Ben had been good to me over the years; years when I did not always produce a real gem of a novel. On the other hand, battling with Sorrabon Publishing, and Ms. Sarah, would bring some pleasure, especially when winning. I think that the immediate thing to do was to start talking to other publishers and see just how marketable I really am. We could address the new publishing firm another day.

Just as we were finishing our drinks and discussing getting another, the house phone rang. We looked at each other wondering if it was for real, or just another 'event'. Soon the phone's answer machine picked up and we heard a voice saying "Sarah Douglas. Call me right away. Today! You missed the deadline I gave you and you'll have serious consequences. You have my number. Call me, you have my number. I'm waiting." Then everything went silent.

"Well," said Stephanie, "we need to save that message. If we ever go to court, those kind of messages are helpful bits of evidence. And...I think I will take another drink." She pushed her martini glass across the dining room table toward me.

My martinis are not nearly as good as Yuri would make for us, but they are passable. Besides, if you drink four or five, they begin to taste better and better. I walked through the kitchen and over to the bar in the library. My mind was still spinning with all the information that Stephanie had bestowed upon me. And she said she wasn't done, yet. Well maybe it would be a good night for Chinese take-out and martinis. Hhhmmm.

Stephanie's cell phone rang. After looking at the caller ID, she answered saying,"Hello, Desmond. Are you at the office, still?" She took the martini and set it on the table in front of her. She then drew a line across the liquid level to show me that I had not filled it as much this time, as last time. "Really?" she took a quick sip before saying," Can we prove that? Do we have anything which would confirm that Ben Haberman was involved in that?" She turned her head toward me to catch my staring at her. "Well, that is enough evidence for U.S. courts to convict. Good detective work, Desmond. Email me copies of what you have, I'll be working from home for a few days, and put the originals in the company safe. Desmond, I owe you a drink or two. Thank you and have a good night." Stephanie ended the call and took a sip of her martini. She winked at me saying, "much better than the last one, but I bet this is not as good as the next one will be."

"Come on, I'm on the edge of my seat. What about Ben Haberman? What, so called, evidence?" I asked.

"Seems your Ms. Sarah and Mr. Haberman have been having an affair for many years." Stephanie said.

"Is that all?" I asked. "That's not a big thing these days." Although it really disappointed me because I had always thought that Ben was a good Catholic, family man who followed the 'straight and narrow.'

"Give me a minute," Stephanie said, "you made this drink

too good to set down. Anyway, Saintly Sarah got pregnant and had to have an 'operation' which Ben paid for. Then, we find that there WERE two VP's above Ben at the corporate level who would have gotten the BIG promotion ahead of Ben. Both of these guys went hiking in the Great Smokey Mountains and had an "accident" when they fell over a five-foot high fence, plunged four hundred feet to their deaths. The surviving hiker in their party was....wait for it...named 'Sarah Douglas.' Am I peaking your interest, yet?" Stephanie laughed a bit and took more sips of her martini.

"Well this is all very interesting, but is it serious enough to hang them with?" I asked. "And what about this 'evidence' you were talking about?"

"Keep filling me full of alcohol, and I'll spill everything." She giggled again. "We also have a little matter of some missing money. Like, several millions of dollars. Somewhere around four million dollars plus. We are still auditing what financials we can get our hands on. Our firm is their second legal group. Sort of a back-up legal/accounting firm. It appears that the Sarah/Ben combo knows about Guido Kiefer's real identity, and black mailed him with that knowledge. They threatened to expose Guido if he didn't leave the Governor's office when his appointed term was over. Then they hired Guido as VP of Finance to help them hide the missing sums of money. Knowing that they could 'out' him at any time, Guido went along with their deal. Plus, they are making it worthwhile for him with large cash bonuses. There was an 'incident' recently where an elderly, retired woman who used to be a bookkeeper at a couple of Sorrabon's subsidiaries, recognized him as a "Keeper" family member. She later remembered he works at Sorrabon and told her son all about him. The son passed this information on to someone before he was killed in a single car traffic accident in Albany, New York. We need to concentrate on finding out more about the missing money, and, as someone once said, "follow the money."

"This gets more, and more interesting by the minute." I said. "And much of this can be proven in a court of law?"

"Not 'much' of it, ALL of it. We have ninety percent verification of everything right now. The only thing we are trying to do now is to find a young couple who were taking nature photos in the Great Smokies. They accidentally took a picture of a woman pushing two unconscious bodies around a five foot fence on the main hiking trail. Once we have copies of their photos, we're home free."

"Really?" I asked. "All this and photos, too?"

"That is what Desmond called to let me know. He was leaving to go meet the couple and pay them for their photos."

Just then the phone rang. I was tempted to answer it but Stephanie's information train was keeping me focused on what she was saying. Just as Stephanie was about to resume talking, the old familiar voice of Sarah Douglas was heard giving the answer machine the following message: "This is Sarah Douglas. I'm phoning you because I really like you and I want to keep you as one of our 'preferred' authors. However, I can no longer wait. Your time has run out and you must now get your finished, final novel into my hands by the tenth of next month. At the end of next month, your relationship with Sorrabon Publishing and any, and all subsidiaries, will end. You will not have publishing for any future works available in New York City and we will work to keep any of your works from ever being distributed. Have a nice…" The message machine ended without anything further.

"Very tempted to pick up the phone and tell Ms. Sarah that we know all about her, Ben and Gilbert's little deals," I told Stephanie. "Tempted, but let's see what we have when we get all our cards together. Then we can do something, I hope."

Just then my cell phone started ringing. I grabbed it off my desk and tried to recall if I had ever talked to someone with the phone number shown on caller ID. Undecided, I answered it with "Hello?" A man's voice was on the other end asking me if I knew a man named Guido Kiefer. Unsure of how to answer I asked why. The man hesitated for a moment, then went on with "Mr. Guido Kiefer is among one-hundred-two passengers who were aboard an Asian Airlines flight 344. That flight disappeared from radar about twenty four hours ago and has not been located since. Mr. Kiefer listed you and this phone number as his 'emergency contact' in case of something happening. We're trying to advise the 'emergency contacts' listed because we believe something has happened. We will contact you at this phone number, but we will also send follow up information to your email address, if desired." I thanked the caller, gave him my personal email address and ended the call.

I looked at Stephanie sipping the last of her martini. She asked who was on the phone. I told her about the man's message and how Gilbert Keeper/Guido Kiefer was missing for over twenty four hours and that he had been aboard a missing Asian Air flight from Singapore to Myanmar. I didn't know, yet, if this situation eliminated a problem, or created a new one. Time would tell.

We decided that one more martini would be great before digging into the Chinese food that had been delivered earlier. I mixed two more and set one down in front of Stephanie. Grey Goose dirty martinis and chicken chow mein. Some days life just doesn't get any better!

CHAPTER 11

Waking up the next morning, I wasn't sure if I should try to move my head, or not. I slowing began a gentle rolling over from my back to my left side. All it took was a move of about an inch and my head exploded. Literally, it seemed like it exploded. I knew then that I had better do this much, much slower before I risked really hurting myself. Slow. Slow and steady, but especially slow.

Finally as I swung my legs over the side of the bed, I noticed that Stephanie's side was empty. It was then that I got a whiff of the aroma of bacon frying somewhere. Must still be dreaming, or I'm having a hangover dream. The 'hangover dream' takes dreaming way beyond its' normal strangeness to a point of making the dreamer unsure if they are dreaming, awake, or even alive. Hangover dreams were akin to having a dream-within-a-dream-within-a-dream. Not that I've had a lot of hangover dreams, but I have included my one experience in book four. Ah, book four. The biggest selling book/novel in the publishing history of Sorrabon. There I go, thinking about work, and Sorrabon Publishing, already, before even getting out of bed.

I grabbed a robe, slippers and my cell phone as I headed downstairs to the aroma, and sound of bacon frying. Sunshine was blasting into the entryway and reflecting off the marble floor, making me wish I had sunglasses on.

"Good morning, Sunshine", came the greeting from Stephanie. "Was it my magnetic personality that drew you out of bed, or the smell of bacon frying?"

"Personality, of course," I replied. "Your personality draws me into bed, as well as out of bed."

Stephanie told me that she would have breakfast ready in about ten minutes, in case I wanted to have some coffee. A good idea, I thought. The coffee, that is.

I visited 'King' Keurig for some dark roast while I checked emails and messages on my cell phone. Mostly advertising emails offering this deal, or that deal. One email from Asian Air saying that their search efforts had now been increased to include resources from several countries, as well as the U.S. Coast Guard, but, so far, there were still no traces of the missing plane. Security camera recordings from the airport in Singapore did confirm that Mr. Guido Kiefer was aboard the plane. Additional information would be forthcoming when available.

Having breakfast with my wife on a sunshiny morning was indeed a treat. We laughed about the sequence of events from the night before. We talked about the possibilities open to us. We talked about getting the 'master seaman' over to train us on proper handling of the yacht. We almost talked more than we ate.

Stephanie pushed her plate away from her, saying "Whew,

I took too much. Way too much. I'll need to go on a good, long run later to work that off." Stephanie had always been a devout runner since about age 10. She talked long and hard trying to get me into doing it. Not much success for her, so far. I'm more of a treadmill-at-a-much-slower-pace, type person. But she loved her long runs along the river, or around town. Westport has a lot of walkways going all around the city that both runners and cyclists love. Made a safer, away from the little bit of traffic environment, for both.

I walked over to 'King' Keurig to brew a second cup of dark roast. After all the martinis that we had last night, the dark roast coffee was certainly a necessity. "I think I will work on finishing my book so that it can be delivered to Ms. Sarah early instead of later. I'm nearly done, anyway, just have a bit more research to do for the conclusion. I'm thinking of using a delivery service, also, rather than my usual method of hand delivery. I no longer have an urge to see Sorrabon Publishing, or their offices." I poured the beautiful second cup of dark roast and added, "A delivery service will avoid me having to endure any rants from Sarah Douglas, and will give me a signed receipt that they received it. I could email it, but I like the idea of a signed receipt."

Stephanie agreed and started clearing away dirty dishes. I told her to leave the dishes and I would take care of them. She thanked me and said she was going to change and go on her run instead.

After clearing away all the dishes, loading the dishwasher to its' full capacity and getting it started on the long cycle, I grabbed my cup of coffee and headed to my office. An obvious advantage of working at home is the ability to work in one's pajamas, or underwear. Pajamas were my uniform of choice today as I started pounding the keys on the way to the novel's finish.

I hadn't noticed that over an hour had passed until Stephanie put her head through the partially opened office door. Asking how I was progressing, she said that she had just finished a really good run. She told me all about the new areas of our city that she had seen on her run. She told me about the beautiful, scenic coastal views when going west instead of her usual easterly route. She also told me about the strangest, elderly woman she had met at a rest stop.

"Her name is Marianna, and she claims to be from Haiti. She is supposed to be some sort of mystic who can foretell the future and read people's minds. At first she seemed a little bit crazy, and scary, but the more we talked, the more believable I found her to be. She was dressed in clothes reminiscent of Goodwill stores; really shabby and not too clean. However, and this is what I found to be strange, she told me all about our house, you, and some things about myself. She knew I am an attorney and part of a big law firm. She knew that you were having problems with a woman who was not your wife. She saw a close friend of yours dead in some water. And...are you ready for this? She told me that our house is cursed. That it has bad, bad mojo because of really bad things that happened here long, long ago. She could not tell exactly what the bad things were, so she didn't say 'murders,' but she knew that what happened involved a family. She finally told me that many bad things would continue to happen in this house until the souls of all those responsible were put to rest. Now you know I do not believe in "mystics," or fortune tellers, or any of those type people who claim to be able to see into the future. I just don't! But, this woman just knew too much. Things that no one other than us could have known."

Stephanie had come through the doorway and into my office by now. I looked at her elevated state of excitement and leaned back in my chair.

"How do you think she knew this much? These things about us? This mystery about our house?" I asked, sipping the last bit of cold coffee from my cup.

"I don't know," Stephanie said, "but she knew FACTS! Facts are what I mostly deal with, and she knew facts. I didn't want to listen and even started to resume my run, but she said too many facts that just compelled me to stay and listen. And then, guess what happened! She got up off the bench we were sitting on, and left. Not just walking off, she ran. Ran as if she were an

Olympic-caliber sprinter! In her baggy old clothes and sandals, she ran! There was no way I was going to catch up with her; I run fast, but not at the speed she was moving. Then she was gone."

"How is your head this morning after all those martinis last night?" I asked with a hint of skepticism therein. "Think maybe this could be some sort of day dream, or something?"

"I know. It sounds stranger than hell, but it happened!" Stephanie replied. "And the thing that I didn't tell you: she knew I had an employee named 'Desmond!' She likes the name because she has a cousin in Haiti whose name is Desmond. Only she pronounced it, "Deezmond". I know how this sounds, but it happened. Really!"

I acknowledge to Stephanie that I believed her, even though I remained skeptical about it all. I thought about everything she had said, thought, about this house and thought about the novel. The novel was going to be my attention for today. "Let's process all of that, and we'll analyze it all later. Right now, I need to finish this bit of research and concentrate on completing this book. I found a bonded, licensed courier service here in Westport that can take the finished book to Sorrabon's offices. Costly, but will be worth it in the end."

Stephanie said she was going to shower and change and do some gardening as it was an absolutely gorgeous day outdoors.

She smiled and headed out the office door and up the stairs. I went back to work on finishing my research and pounding the keyboard.

Book finished, I phoned the courier company and let them take it to the city and hand it over to Sorrabon Publishing, and Ms. Sarah Douglas. I had listed Sarah, or her assistant Bruce, as the only people who were acceptable recipients at Sorrabon. Now the 'finish line' with Sorrabon was becoming more visible.

I opened emails on my desktop computer and saw two recent ones from Asian Airlines. I quickly opened the older email and found it only continued with most of what had been said before. The more recent email was much more interesting. It said that they believed that Mr. Guido Kiefer, American businessman, had been found alive. In critical condition with life-threatening injuries, but alive. They said they knew that distance could prevent an easy and immediate flight to Bangkok, Thailand, to identify the passenger as Mr. Kiefer, so they asked me to contact their New York City offices to arrange a 'Skype' type of call with the medical center in Bangkok. Mr. Kiefer's condition, at last report, was critical and time could be of the essence.

The email included additional information about whom I should speak with, and their toll–free phone numbers. They also said that Mr. Kiefer's personal laptop computer, and several business papers had been recovered with other passengers' belongings off the coast of Phang-Nga, a province in Thailand.

I quickly went upstairs to find Stephanie toweling off from her shower, and told her about the emails.

"What's your thinking?" she asked. "Obviously, a flight to Bangkok is out of the question. Especially after what we now know about Gilbert, er, Guido. Do you want to set up their 'Skype' type thing and do you want me to go with you if you do that?"

I thought for a few seconds. "Yes, I think the 'Skype' type phone call is the best way to handle it, and, yes I would like you to be there. If only to help keep me from saying the wrong thing. I'll call their offices in the city and make the arrangements. What sort of commitments do you have coming up in the next few days?"

Stephanie dropped the towel and walked into the bedroom to retrieve her cell phone. Checking her calendar on the iPhone, she told me she was almost completely clear until next Thursday afternoon. Then she had a meeting with the Vanderbilts to go over some 'new' legal matters. I told her I would take care of it. I couldn't help but just stand and stare at Stephanie's gorgeous nakedness, and remember the last time we had both worn only our skin in bed.

"Easy there, fellow, you have phone calls to make, and your PJ's are beginning to bulge," she said.

I laughed and did my 'non-military' about face to leave the bedroom and return to my office downstairs. Before I reached the phone on my desk, it rang. I saw that the caller ID registered a local Westport phone number that looked a little familiar. I picked up the receiver and said, "Hello." A deep man's voice responded. "Yes, this is he." Seems that the caller was a fellow named 'Johnathan Kauffman'. He is the master seaman from the marina, and wanted to let me know that he would be leaving on vacation at the end of next week. Was I interested in his coming by the house to instruct me, and my wife, on the operation and safety features of my Yacht. If we could not do it one day next week, then we would have to wait over six weeks until his return. Johnathan also informed me that the other local master seaman, Michael McGuire, had left Connecticut and returned to his native Ireland. But Michael only had 20 years of sea experience, whereas Johnathan had nearly forty-eight years; twenty years as a master. I asked him how he started, and he replied as a bait boy on a fishing trawler. Working himself up to a 'master' level, he then spent years on other types of ocean-going vessels in the Merchant Marines, and in the Navy during the war. It was tough for me to NOT go after the joke material that laid within Johnathan's credentials: that of his working his way up from a 'bait boy,' to a 'master baiter.' But I overcame the urge and grabbed my phone to check my calendar. I asked Johnathan how much time he would need. He replied that he always liked to have a full day available, say from nine in the morning to five or six at night, but could do a

126

shortened version if we were pressed for time.

Stephanie was walking past my office doorway, with clothes on, when I called to her.

I told her who was on the phone, and why he was calling. Asked how would Wednesday be with her to have Johnathan come by and give us the lessons. She asked if the lessons would involve any actual sailing, or not. Something I had not thought of, so I put the question to Johnathan.

He said, "Of course." That is why he liked to do a full day's instructions, so that three-to-four hours of teaching the "this-does-that" could be followed with three-to-four hours of actual sailing experience. He added that we are blessed to have some of the best winds and most beautiful coastal scenery of anywhere right here in Connecticut, so, "why not go sailing?" We all agreed on Wednesday as the day Stephanie and I went to classes.

I phoned Asian Airlines, explained who I am and why I was calling, to a very nice Asian lady. She already had my name and cell phone number on a list and was expecting me to call. We went over how we would do the call and what Asian Airline's purpose was in this. As it turned out, Thursday morning, early, was available and worked perfectly with Stephanie's schedule. We set it up for then. Please bring photo ID with us for identification purposes.

CHAPTER 12

The following days were great. Stephanie worked from home, I did a lot of research for another idea I had for my 'next' book, Stephanie did a lot of gardening, we ate dinners out at different eateries every night, and we both went clothes shopping for what Stephanie called our "yachting duds." Everything both of us did paid off well. I had enough facts and material for at least two more books, the front and rear yards were beautiful because of Stephanie's 'green thumb', and we both were, to put it mildly, going to be 'fashion icons' in our 'yachting duds.'

The day of instruction with Johnathan Kauffman went well and we finished the morning session regarding the boat early. Since the painter had not finished painting the ship's name on the stern and both bow locations, Stephanie suggested that she fix lunch for the four of us before we set out on our 'sail'. It's funny but everyone uses the term 'sail', even when you have a twin-engine diesel powered vessel such as ours. Johnathan thanked Stephanie and thought that to be a good idea, although the boat had a very nice, fully equipped kitchen aboard and meals could be prepared while 'sailing.' The painter thanked Stephanie but said he had only about thirty minutes more of work until he was done and then he had to return to the sales yard to finish two boats parked there. So the three of us sat on the patio at the rear of the house and enjoyed soup, sandwich halves, and some cream puffs that Stephanie bought in town yesterday.

The painter waved good bye when he left the dock saying that everything was done and dry and ready for sailing. The "Stephanie's Joy" was ready for sea.

Master seaman Johnathan Kauffman was absolutely correct! As I eased the boat away from our dock, pointed the compass due south-south-west down the Saugatuck River, I marveled at just how beautiful everything is. Passing Judy Point on the west bank we saw a group of young boys sitting while trying their luck at fishing. As we passed the Westport Longshore Park on the east banks of the river, we all waved at a group of people standing near Hendrick's Point. I paid close, nervous, attention to every detail that was occurring on the instruments, radio, sonar, and the engine gauges. Everything seemed to be going along exactly as it should.

As we passed the Yacht Club at Cedar Point, all the boats there, along with the yacht club offices, and even cars parked in their parking lot began sounding their horns. It sounded like either the fourth of July, or the world's largest protest going on. Johnathan told Stephanie and I that he had notified the Commandant of the yacht club that we would be taking our maiden cruise aboard our new boat, and that they were all sounding off to welcome us to their world of boating. It gave me chills as we waved back at them to show our appreciation.

The next three hours passed by like thirty minutes. Johnathan had me set a course for the Peck Ledge Lighthouse which was slightly southwest of Cockenoe Island. Then he had Stephanie take the helm and gave her several destinations among the grouping of islands to sail to. She did very well and was obviously very pleased with herself.

"I may have found my calling", she told Johnathan and I. "This could be my new occupation." About that time a bunch of college boys went flying past in a speed boat which sent a huge series of waves into us broadside. This made the boat rock back-and-forth and made Stephanie squeal a bit. Johnathan told her to hold steady and ride the waves out, but each rocking motion made Stephanie squeal more. "You're doing fine," Johnathan told her as the last little wave dissipated. As the rocking lessened, Stephanie eased the engines controls forward and told us that she wanted an idea how the boat would feel at a higher speed. She really seemed to be having a good time commanding this large boat. Maybe she had found herself a new occupation, but for now I hope she sticks with the law.

We stopped at the yacht club for refueling since Johnathan said they had about the lowest diesel cost of anyone within one-hundred miles. I asked Johnathan if he wanted us to let him off here, but he said no that he had a car parked at our house and wanted to see how I handled the re-docking at our dock. While we were filling the fuel tanks, a man came speed walking down the pier toward our boat.

"Hi, there," he said, "I'm Miles Stanton, the Commandant of the Yacht Club and I brought your application with me to give to you." We shook hands and I introduced Miles to my wife. He asked how Johnathan was treating us and I told him that he was certainly a credit to sailing and the sea. His knowledge about sailing, and this model boat, was amazing and extremely helpful and interesting. Miles welcomed us as he handed me the membership application. "Simply fill in the areas indicated and return to us. We've already signed it by the five members who will be sponsoring you two. Stephanie, did I hear correctly? You are an attorney? We need a good attorney within the club to review things for us and advise us on an occasional matter. I hope we can count on your services. Well I have to run, I'm keeping my wife waiting and we're having dinner at her brother's house in Boston tonight. Nice meeting both of you and look forward to seeing you both at next month's meeting. Johnathan, take care of our new members. Good sailing."

With that, Miles Stanton scurried off down the pier to the yacht club's offices. I looked at Stephanie as she shrugged her shoulders and gave me a slight smile.

Johnathan said that our fuel tanks were full and we should head for our dock. I paid for the fuel and shut everything down on the dock. Starting the twin engines gave me a thrill that I had not had in a long time. Johnathan showed me how to throttle the two engines to make maneuvering alongside our dock much easier. I made a couple dockings before letting Stephanie try it. She did very well and felt that one try was sufficient for now. We secured the boat and made certain everything was locked and bolted. Thanking Johnathan, we offered to buy him dinner if he had the time. He thanked us but declined our offer. Seems he has a sick wife at home and he had to go relieve his sister who was staying with her during the day. Off he went.

Stephanie and I decided that we would get some pizza and pasta take-out and bring it home. We have an early morning appointment with Asian Airlines to try to identify Guido Kiefer, and Stephanie has her afternoon meeting. A good night's sleep could help us recharge our batteries and ready for tomorrow.

The following morning was overcast and the weather person on the news said there was a chance of off and on showers during the day. Both Stephanie and I got ready and headed out to the train station. Umbrella in hand, I locked the car and met Stephanie on the station platform. This time the train was not on time, but arrived twenty minutes late. Fortunately we did not have a firm time when we had to arrive at Asian Airlines. With an eleven hour difference between Bangkok and New York City, everything had to be worked out when we were available. So Stephanie and I used the travel time aboard the train to review yesterday's training with Johnathan aboard our boat. Stephanie wanted to stock the boat with non-perishable food items, some beverages, and take it out again this weekend. She already had made a mental list of towels, blankets and other needed items from our house that we could use aboard the boat when sailing. She thought that the more we took the boat out cruising, the better sailors we would be.

She asked if I thought I would be going to the upcoming yacht club meeting. I told her that I wasn't thinking that far ahead; there were too many other matters to plan for before that meeting. Besides, we were NOT official members, yet.

The taxi ride from Grand Central Station to the offices of Asian Airlines was short and easy. Their receptionist was very helpful and courteous upon our arriving. She phoned someone in the back offices that we were waiting and asked if we would like some water. We both thanked her for the offer, but said no.

Shortly, an attractive, well dressed Asian woman of about forty years of age came through the reception room door and greeted us. She apologized for her delay and asked if we would follow her. She led Stephanie and I through a set of double doors and into a huge inner office where dozens and dozens of people were scurrying around everywhere. We walked down a long aisle to a conference room at the other end. We entered and were asked to sit in adjoining chairs opposite a group of seven people seated on the opposite side of the long table. One man introduced himself as Mr. Hansei Matsumo, the head of technology and the lead person in the investigation of this horrible event. He seemed to intentionally refrain from using words like 'tragic' or 'accident'. He said that he had already talked to the hospital administrators in Bangkok, and they were trying to set things up there. Unfortunately with an eleven hour difference between New York City and Bangkok everything took more time.

Finally, after waiting about thirty-five minutes, the screen on the wall above a lectern went bright with color. A room filled with color and bamboo objects came into clearer focus. Nothing happened for another four, or five, minutes and then a smiling man with a white surgeon's cap on, stepped in front of the camera. He introduced himself as the head of surgery at the central medical center where the 'survivors' of the plane crash had been taken. He said that the man whom they believed to be Mr. Guido Kiefer had been in surgery earlier today and that he may not be completely coherent now. Seems they were wheeling him in on a surgery gurney from his 'space,' to here where the camera is. About that time, a group of people pushing a gurney and some holding bottles in the air came into camera range. There on the gurney lay a man completely bandaged on every part of his head. Both hands and arms were covered with gauge bandages so that no skin was showing anywhere.

The doctor who identified himself as head of surgery asked

us if we could identify this man. Both Stephanie and I stared at each other with a puzzled look on our faces. I got up and walked up to the big screen TV on the wall with hopes of getting a clearer and better view. Nope. It was impossible to tell who they had bandaged so completely.

"I'm sorry but I cannot tell who that person is, I told the group. "There is no part of his face visible to us."

The head of surgery said that it would not be possible for them to remove any bandages as most of the covered areas were badly burned by a fire aboard the plane. He then said that the man had a small eagle-like bird tattoo high on his left shoulder, and asked if that would help us.

I tried to explain to the Bangkok group, as well as all people in our conference room, that I only knew Guido Kiefer from Grad school and from some business over the years. Guido had been one member of our wedding party, but he and I were not close, close friends. I had never seen him without being completely clothed, so I did not know if he had tattoos, or not. I would need to see his unbandaged face to be able to tell if it was him.

Everyone in our conference room, and in Bangkok huddled in their respective groups to talk. And talk, and talk. Seems both groups had much to discuss among themselves. After eight to ten minutes, the Bangkok group seemed to panic and said that

Mr. Kiefer was having some sort of medical problem and they needed to get him back to an examination area to determine what was wrong. With that they all raced off pushing the gurney in front of them.

Mr. Matsumo asked me if there was anything about Mr. Kiefer that would help to make a positive identification. I repeated to him that I did not know Guido Kiefer that well and unless I could see his face I could not make an identification. I am amazed that he even listed me as his emergency contact person since I knew so little about him. He looked at the other people in his group, then rose from his chair and thanked both of us for our time. Asian Airlines would continue to update us with all information that they receive on Mr. Kiefer via email, as before.

The airline's Singapore office had shipped all belongings identified as Mr. Kiefer's direct to us at our home. They hoped that this was acceptable. When I asked if he knew what the items were, or how many items there were, he did not. He only knew that there were five people whose belongings had been retrieved and identified. He knew one item was Mr. Kiefer's laptop computer, and he had been told that there were some 'computer parts', also. Beyond that he did not know anything.

Stephanie and I talked with the group for another fifteen minutes before leaving. We walked out of the office building and into a light rainfall. This time I remembered to bring an umbrella, and I quickly put it to good use.

We decided to grab something small to eat for lunch before Stephanie headed off to her office and her afternoon meetings.

We found a small café on a side street and it had one remaining table open. We ordered sandwiches from the menu painted on the wall, and ordered beer from the list painted on the ceiling. Apparently if you're not able to read the list on the ceiling, then you're too drunk to have another beer. We ate our food and talked about the morning's events, especially as it regarded Guido Kiefer. There was no way that anyone could have identified the person on the gurney there in Bangkok.

After we finished our sandwiches and beers Stephanie decided that she should leave for her office. There was just enough time for her to get there, gather some papers and prepare for the meeting with her clients. I told Stephanie that I was going to contact an old school buddy who had left a message on my cell phone regarding a new publishing firm that he thought I might be interested in. He said that the firm had some notable names already under contract and was looking for more authors. He had more information that he would give me when we talked. I would find a quiet place and give him a call for more info.

As we left the small café, rain was coming down harder. I

hailed a taxi for us and gave the driver the address of Stephanie's offices.

When we arrived at Stephanie's office building, we hugged, kissed goodbye and she made a mad dash for the entrance. I told the taxi driver that the next stop would be Grand Central Station. And a nice quiet corner therein.

It had been a couple weeks since we went to Asian Airlines for the meeting. The investigation into the disappearance of their airplane, and its' passengers continued without significant results. One-by-one the few people who had been found alive, or nearly dead, off the coast of Thailand, had passed away. Our concern was the man thought to be Guido Kiefer, had undergone many operations to correct a series of serious, life-threatening, events. He still had not been positively identified. Dental records did not exist on Guido Kiefer, or Gilbert Keeper. The box of personal belongings had arrived from the hospital in Bangkok, Thailand, but still set in the entryway where it had originally been dropped. Unopened, the box did not have a high priority with me. Something I would get to...eventually.

Stephanie was spending more time working from home, only going into the city for partner's meetings and an occasional 'preferred client' meeting. Her sister had even canceled their last two monthly 'dinners on the Green.' She felt like she was doing better work at home than she did with all the interruptions, and office politics, that went on in the firm's offices.

We took "Stephanie's Joy" out at every opportunity. Sometimes for only two or three hours, other times for the whole day. We had even taken a weekend cruise east up the coast to Gooseberry Island, Rhode Island. A weekend cruise that was nearly perfect with weather, food, martinis, company and sights to see. The more we 'sailed,' the more we enjoyed it and both felt that the cost of the "Stephanie's Joy" was worth every cent; especially Stephanie. She had gotten the boat outfitted with all the linens, food, beverages, and other necessary items that one could imagine; everything which made a day on the water, as comfortable as any day at home.

Stephanie's law firm had completed a major technology upgrade recently, which made her even more able to complete her every task from home. She used their network for research, for corresponding with partners, and for just about every task she needed. This enabled her to stop procuring books for her legal library at home. She now enjoyed her home office more and more because she could display her collection of small works of art, instead of volumes, and volumes of law books.

I had contacted a former school friend about joining a new publishing firm. He was not an author himself, but did represent a few who had signed contracts with the new firm, and were very pleased with the arrangements. I sent a list of my previous book titles, and estimated numbers sold for each. I also sent an extract of my 'ideas' for my next novel, which they really liked. They boosted my ego when they responded that no establishing of credentials was necessary for me; I was a well known entity whose name alone was a sufficient credential.

I had also been contacted by the state university about possibly becoming a professor of journalism. While this was not a position I had thought of, it did hold some real attraction for me. It certainly was one of those things that I had thought of at one point in my career after a modicum of success had been achieved. Apparently, on one of our little sojourns to Massachusetts to have lunch with Stephanie's clients, the Vanderbilts, one of them had decided to recommend me to a friend within the Connecticut Department of Education. I sent my resume to them and had set up an appointment for an interview. Sometimes it is good to have contacts.

The days were a mixture of sunny, hot days that were spent 'lunching' on the patio or the boat, and cloudy, blustery days when working inside at home was really welcomed. Some days were also filled with wondering just where the future laid. I was nearing the interview time with the State Board of Education for the professorship with mixed feelings. I speculated that this position could require much more time away from the house, the boat, and Stephanie, than I would like. I had come to relish my 'lazy man's schedule' as Stephanie referred to it, and did not want that to change. It put me in quite a quandary.

I kept walking past the box of Guido's belongings sitting where it had been placed upon arriving, and decided it finally had come time to open it and inspect its' contents. If for no other reason than to get the ugly cardboard box, with its' very strange writing, out of the front entryway of the house. I found a 'box knife' in my tool drawer and cut the heavy cord and sealing tape that kept the contents in place. Upon opening the top flaps I found Guido's laptop computer nicely wrapped in heavy, waterproof paper to protect it. Also inside the box was filled with peanuts; not the Styrofoam packing 'peanuts' we're used to seeing, but actual peanuts. I guess Thailand has a lot of peanuts available and not much Styrofoam. Anyway, the rest of the items were varied and mixed: a belt, tie, three manila folders full of papers, a passport, seven large capacity memory sticks, another passport, and four bullets. The more I looked at the lineup of items on the dining room table, the more confused I became. Why two passports? Why the four bullets? Why? Why? Why?

I decided to cut the cardboard carton into pieces and drop them into the recycle bin. We always did our part for the environment by recycling. I did or I would really hear about it from Stephanie. The assortment of weird stuff from Guido's carton could stay on the table until I was in a frame of mind to examine everything.

I did more work in my office until Stephanie came home. She walked through the front door with a tall, very muscular looking black man behind her. Stephanie usually came home through the back door as it was closer to her office where she would drop files and her attaché. She told the man to have a seat in the family room and she would be right there.

"I'm home," she called out heading for her office. "Are you in your office or upstairs?"

"I'm here in my office," I answered. "Did I hear we have company?"

By the time I had asked the question, she was poking her head through my office door. "Hi, there. Working hard?" she asked

"Or hardly working?," I added. I rose from my chair to go give her a kiss. "Did you bring someone with you?" I asked, as I also gave her a hug.

"Yes, I did. I want you to come meet Desmond Winston, my firm's chief investigator. He's the fellow who got all that information for you on Guido. Come on out of your 'cave'," Stephanie said as she turned to walk away.

I followed her into the family room to see a huge body of a man rising from a chair. He must have been six-feet-four, or more, and very well built. He extended his hand to shake hands as I got near.

"Hello, sir, It is indeed a pleasure to finally meet you. Your wife always talks about you; always in very glowing terms," Desmond said.

"Hello, Desmond," I said, realizing that my hand and forearm were aching from the grip and strength of Mr. Desmond. "Likewise. My wife has very high praise for the work you do, and we especially appreciate your digging up the data on that Guido Kiefer. Good job!"

"Believe it or not, Desmond has some more 'dirt' on your friend Guido." Stephanie added. "I told him I would buy him a drink or two for the extra work he's done for us. Then, I find out that Desmond loves barbeque. So I promised him a barbeque dinner downtown at 'Bobby Q's Barbeque Grill. He jokingly said that he might kill for great barbeque. At least I hope he was joking."

"Sounds great to me. I should probably change into something more formal for BBQ like an old shirt and jeans," I said. "Desmond, you're going to stand out in that suit and tie and I'm sure that nothing in my closet would fit you."

Desmond explained that he had dropped a bag in the entryway which had his 'barbeque caliber' clothes in it. It seemed that Desmond was on his way to Boston to see his younger sister and her family, so he had everything he needed for a casual dinner. He declined my offer of a drink saying that he would wait to peruse Bobby Q's well-known bourbon offerings. I excused myself to go upstairs to change.

A few minutes later Stephanie joined me in our bedroom to change into some more appropriate clothes. While changing into jeans and a floppy shirt, she asked me what the mess on the dining room table was all about. I told her that I had finally gotten the carton of Guido's things unboxed and now I had to go through it all to see what it is. I told Stephanie about the two passports and the four bullets. She looked at me with a bit of disbelief.

Clothes changed we both went downstairs to see Desmond hanging his 'working' clothes on a hanger in the hallway closet. His muscular build was even more visible when he was standing there in casual clothes. He could have passed for a defensive back for the New England Patriots.

"Ready?," I asked Desmond as I headed to lock and bolt the front door. We would go out the back and use Stephanie's car which she always pulled back near the garage. After Desmond and Stephanie went outside, I set the Alarm system and made certain that the automatic sounds and light systems were activated. We then drove downtown to Bobby Q's

Dinner was delicious. Desmond couldn't believe how extensive Bobby Q's offering of bourbons was and ended up having a sampler of several that he had not tried before. Seems Desmond is a connoisseur of fine bourbons, among other things. Between the excellent drinks, great barbeque meats, delicious side dishes, and Desmond's loving the choices in bourbons, we were unsure if we would be able to walk out of Bobby Q's at all. We learned a great deal about Mr. Desmond Winston during dinner: he is six-feet-six and a half, was a body builder and instructor in Tai Quan Do to help pay his way through undergrad school, was an All-American defensive back at Oklahoma State, played pro football for the Dallas Cowboys for four years before a severe auto accident ended his playing career. He got into detective work because of a cousin of his being killed in a drive-by shooting in St. Louis, Mo. The killing left his uncle without someone to assist with private investigations. His uncle needed someone big enough to be his sort of body guard, and Desmond needed work. Desmond took to this type of work and really liked it. Working for a firm like Stephanie's was like gravy for the biscuits.

We discussed Guido and the additional information that Desmond had been able to gather. I asked Desmond if he had any idea why Guido would have two passports; he said he did but it was in the papers that he had given to Stephanie. He said that Guido was playing both sides of a very dangerous game; that game being that Guido was covering large thefts of monies from Sorrabon Corporation by Ben Haberman and Sarah Douglas, and then selling that information along with some bits of evidence to another publishing company rumored to want to purchase the entire family of Sorrabon subsidiaries. I processed that bit of information before asking Desmond what that meant.

"Essentially it means that Guido Kiefer is playing Russian roulette with a gun that has five bullets in it" answered Desmond. "He is in a lose-lose situation, and is not going to win. The other publishing company he is dealing with is a Chinese company and it is completely controlled by their government. He may think that he has control of situations he is involved in, but they have total control."

I asked Desmond if he was aware that Guido was either near death in a hospital in Bangkok, Thailand, or is missing completely. He said he was. I asked him if there was anything threatening to national security. He said that he asked a friend of his at NSA the same question and his friend said he couldn't answer. I told Desmond about some of the items I had taken out of the box including the four bullets. He raised his eyebrows and said ,"wow!" He asked if there was time to look at the items at our house. I said I would pay the bill and we could leave when he was ready. He was ready.

Stephanie, Desmond, and I went in the back door of our house after I turned alarms, sensors and the sound array off, and went immediately to the dining room table. Stephanie offered to make tea for anyone interested, but we both declined. Desmond took the laptop computer out of protective paper coverings and tried to start it up. Nothing happened. He then looked at the array of memory sticks and noticed that one had written it "sensitive". He examined the laptop again and then smiled saying "this is an Apple product, and so is mine. I bet my power chord, and such, will work on this." With that Desmond went over and opened his duffle bag and removed a ziplock bag of wires. He took one out and plugged it into the laptop. Plugging the other end into a outlet, he smiled big when the computer went on sounding its' gentle chime. Rapidly we had a bright screen full of folders, pictures and such. Far too much to examine in the few minutes we had before Desmond had to leave to catch his train. Desmond started looking into the folders one-by-one, and opening the pictures to see what they held. He poured over image after image, and all we kept hearing is, "wow!" He asked if we could move the laptop into my office so that we could print copies of some of what he was finding. I told him we could probably print from here if he wanted to. I gave him a card with the network information on it and 'bingo', Desmond was printing!

Desmond looked up at me as the sound of the printer churning out printed pages came from my office and said, "This is unbelievable! Guido may have been an educated person, but he was not very smart! He has left Excel files with dollar-by-dollar amounts of what was being stolen by Ben and Sarah. He's left photo images of accounts, account numbers, passwords, and even a few pictures of the fronts of banks they deposited stolen monies into. We could have enough evidence right here to put all of them away for a good long time." He then started putting a memory stick into the USB connection on the laptop and reading the contents of each.

"What do you mean when you say 'all of them'? Don't you mean Ben and Sarah?" asked Stephanie.

"No. There are at least four more people involved in this, also. Their names, addresses, how much they were paid and when, and their jobs within the corporation are all shown in the main file on the laptop." Desmond continued looking at the memory sticks' contents. "This is so much bigger than just your friend Guido. This is international now."

Stephanie looked at me and asked, "What do you think we should do? Should we get the police involved?"

"First thing I want to do is to make copies of everything, and I mean everything that we have here. We do not know where this may go, if anywhere, and we do not need to have our only copy of evidence, or proof, disappear." I then looked at the clock on the dining room wall, and then at my watch to confirm. Looking at Desmond I said to him, "Desmond, I'm afraid you just missed the last northbound train to Boston. You can't continue you trip to your sisters' place until tomorrow."

Desmond smiled at both of us saying that his sister

expected to see him only when he showed up on her front porch. Stephanie said that she would put extra blankets on the bed in the guest room, and get some fresh towels for the guest bathroom. Desmond thanked her and said that he would really like to start making copies of everything if I had blank memory sticks and enough paper for printing. I assured him I did.

As the hours rolled by, Desmond and I continued to pour through the papers in the manila folders, all the data on the memory sticks, and every file on the laptop. We made copies of everything we had and put our copies in my office safe. It was well after four in the morning, and both Desmond and I were just beat. I showed him where the guest room was at, and the adjoining bathroom and asked him if he needed anything. He said "no" and I asked him if he wanted me to wake him at any certain time. He said he would just grab a couple hours sleep and get up. I thanked Desmond very much for all his work and help with Guido's 'stuff'. I said that Stephanie and I owed him another dinner.

"Darn right you do. Bobby Q's and bourbon! What a combo! Get some sleep yourself and I'll see you in a couple hours," Desmond said as he opened his duffel bag to take something out.

I was glad that Stephanie had gone to bed hours ago. She would be up bright and early to take her morning run along the river. I went back into my office to make certain everything was secured for the night. It was then that I noticed the flashing 'message' light on the phone answering machine. I thought about checking the message now, and quickly changed my mind. I would get to it after coffee in the morning. Some things can wait.

Before I started up to our bedroom, I went into the laundry room and got an empty plastic bin from a stack of them and put all of Guido's things into it.

Now off to bed!

CHAPTER 13

It felt as though I had only blinked my eyes rather than shutting them and falling asleep for a couple of hours. But that's what happened. It was six-forty-five when the sound of the house phone, ringing unmercifully, awakened me from the sleep. Cruel, cruel awakening as I jumped out of bed and tried to find enough vision to reach for the phone in our bedroom.

"Hello?" I muttered to something. "Yes, it is. Who is this?" It appears that the eleven hour time difference between Bangkok and Connecticut didn't matter to the doctors at the medical center there. A doctor, someone, was calling to update me on what they had found out about the surviving passengers. The search for the missing plane was continuing with only occasional findings of clothing, personal items, and a part from the plane, itself. But the real reason for calling me was to let me know that they had positively identified their patient as a Jim Hanover from Los Angeles, California. Seems Mr. Hanover was an actor who was flying to Myanmar to take part in the filming of a movie. However, Mr. Hanover did not survive his major injuries. We continued to discuss the ways in which they had made positive identification, and how much they appreciated our efforts to assist them.

I was asking the caller what they knew about Guido Kiefer when Stephanie came through the bedroom heading for the shower. She had completed her morning run and was not slowing down to ask questions.

The doctor's tone softened as his voice dropped lower saying how sorry they were, but Mr. Kiefer was now listed among the dead and missing passengers. Since no more bodies had been found yet, they had to assume that he, along with the other passengers, were dead. A representative of the airlines would be calling me to update me more. We thanked each other for the call, even though I really didn't mean it because I would have preferred a phone call at a later hour.

I filled Stephanie in on what was discussed during the phone call as she finished showering and dried off. She asked some questions about how they had made the positive identification of this fellow and I told her they had found pictures and photo ID from the plane which matched photos the hospital took when they admitted him. Also, they were finally able to get a finger print match from his documents.

As Stephanie put on her jeans and blouse she asked what this meant about Guido. I told her that they now presumed Guido, along with the other missing passengers, to be dead. No other survivors had been found.

"Desmond is downstairs in the kitchen having coffee if you're wondering. Guess he has been up for almost an hour." She said.

I grabbed my jeans and shirt, threw cold water in my face

and headed off to the kitchen.

Desmond's smile, at least this early in a morning following a very short night before, was just too damn bright and big. I said 'hello' to him and mumbled something about being sorry that the phone rang so early. He said that he had been up long before the phone rang trying out my Keurig machine. He had decided that he would definitely be buying one of those, he said. He liked the single cup idea for coffee, teas, or whatever.

Stephanie joined us for her morning tea and biscotti, and asked about what we found in Guido's things. We sipped coffee, tea, dipped our biscotti and filled Stephanie in on all our discoveries regarding Guido's belongings.

"Appears that Mr. Guido was quite a fellow," she said. "What should we do with all this information, now that we have it? Do we go to the police? Or, do we confront Ben Haberman and Sarah Douglas?"

Desmond already had his opinions ready when he said, "I would like to contact a close friend of mine who works for the state's Attorney General's office and see what he recommends. I would be hesitant to confront Ben or Sarah directly, as we don't know how they would react. It could be dangerous given their personalities. We also have a foreign, government-sponsored company involved in this mess, so I think the State Department should be informed. I can do that, first thing

Monday morning, if you like."

I agreed and thanked Desmond for his offer to sort of spearhead things. Stephanie agreed and said the she would discuss this with her partners to get approval for full use of all her firm's resources, if necessary.

Desmond gathered his clothes and personal items together and we headed off for the train station. Still having over a half hour before the Boston bound train was due, we stood on the platform and talked with Desmond about how things would proceed. He felt very strongly that the more we stayed distant from whatever happens, the better for all of us. Both Stephanie and I agreed, especially since I was being considered for a professorship at State. UCONN did not always have a great sense of humor.

The train arrived, Desmond boarded and headed off for Boston, and his sister's house.

Stephanie and I returned to the house, and although the urge to go back to bed was great within me, I decided to grab a couple folders full of papers and go down to the boat and clean some brass. I grabbed a cup of Keurig dark roast and two folders crammed full of papers and stuff, and headed for the boat.

Stephanie 'gardened', and I 'boated.' Good, relaxing ways to start a weekend morning. As I sat on the upper deck of our boat I read through page after page of emails sent from Ben or

Sarah through some coded server somewhere, to Guido giving instructions on how to handle their stolen funds. Guido also had emails from a foreign national with an Asian last name that confirmed receipt of copies of transfers and 'other significant documents.' The more I read through Guido's papers, the less I felt I knew this person, and the angrier I became that this mess had entered our lives. Then I found something new: newspaper clippings that covered the arrest of someone named Anthony Keeper. Seems this fellow was arrested and charged with murder in the case of a prominent Chicago lawyer whose parents had been involved with the "great Keefer Murder Case in Connecticut." Within the article was a reference to a brother named Gerald, but no other mention of him. Apparently Guido's , or Gerald's, brother was now serving a life sentence without possibility of parole in one of Illinois's finer prison/hotels.

The more I read through papers, and newspaper clippings, the less I really knew about Guido, or Gerald, or anyone else. As my eyes got heavier and heavier, I decided to stretch out on the couch cushions on the top deck and enjoy the warmth of the sun.

CHAPTER 14

Monday morning arrived like we were leading runners in a half-marathon, approaching the finish line. Phones were ringing, email-notification-sounds were going off on both our cell phones, as well as my computer sounding like it was in a bell-ringing competition. And winning. And while both Stephanie and I were on our cell phones, someone delivered a package to the front door. Keeping this pace up could bring martini time a lot earlier.

The new publishing company, Marathon Media, was offering a very generous contract for my next novel, with options and bonuses that increased for each novel thereafter. UCONN had sent a 'package' to me offering me a teaching position within their languages department, which also had some very nice 'perks' with it in addition to just teaching at UCONN.

Stephanie was on a conference call with all the partners of the law firm explaining some of the facts regarding this situation with Sorrabon Corporation. Unknown to Stephanie, one of the newer partners had just been elected to the Board of Directors at Sorrabon, and asked to be excused from this, and any subsequent, discussions regarding the firm or any subsidiaries. Stephanie continued giving little 'snippets' of information to the remaining partners before turning the topic over to the senior partner for discussion. The questions were many and blunt regarding Stephanie's reasons, and the effect on her husband, her, and the law firm.

Finally, after an hour and twenty minutes of talking, the senior partner called for a vote. There was only one dissenting vote cast. The partners gave full, complete use of all the firm's resources to us to use in whatever way that was needed.

Stephanie thanked all her partners, said her farewells and ended the conference call. She felt very good that all her partners, except one, were willing to go along with what she and I needed the firm for.

As we were eating some lunch, later, Desmond called and asked if we could do either a 'Skype call' or, if better, do a 'Facetime' call and talk. I voted for the 'Facetime' option since both Stephanie and I could be in my office, or hers, and have any needed reference materials close by.

Desmond agreed, suggested my office since I had Guido's things there, and said he, and a friend of his, would be calling back via 'Facetime' at half past the hour.

Okay. We finished lunch, cleared the dishes, and got my desktop computer started and running. I checked the Logitech HD camera on the top of the monitor, and cleared away some miscellaneous items laying around in the background.

"Concerned about the background?" Stephanie asked. "It's

Desmond, not your job interview."

"Just want everything to look good. Wonder if I should apply some touch-up make-up," I mused.

Stephanie laughed at me as the phone started ringing. I checked caller ID to confirm that it was Desmond, but did not recognize the caller's number. Finally I decided to answer it and get rid of the caller before Desmond tried to get through.

"Hello," I said. "Oh, hello. Why are YOU calling?" To my shock it was Sarah Douglas calling. It had been so long since I had talked to her I had forgotten her phone number. Seems Sarah has a friend who works at Asian Airlines, and this friend had informed Sarah a few weeks back that one of her close sorority friends had been killed in the 'missing plane incident.' Sarah had gotten the listing of missing, and dead passengers and noticed the name of Guido Kiefer on it. She said she remembered my mentioning a Guido Kiefer once during a conversation and wanted to offer her condolences if it was my friend. Since I knew for a fact that I had never, not once, mentioned Guido's name to Sarah, I knew that she was lying. Lying through her teeth, but I had to control myself.

"Really?" I said. "I heard about the missing plane and all those people being killed, but I don't know anyone who would be on board a flight in that part of the world."

"So, you didn't get word from the airlines that your friend

Guido was killed?" Sarah asked. "My friend was wrong, then, when she said otherwise."

"No, I didn't. And I didn't consider Guido a friend. He was just a guy from grad school that I had lots of business dealings with; some good, some not-so-good. He was one of my groomsmen at our wedding, and then we lost touch with each other."

"Then you weren't having dinner with Guido in Hartford one evening when an elderly woman created a scene in the Capital Grill?" Sarah asked.

Suddenly this woman knew too much. Time to end this and get away from her cross-examination.

"Sarah, thank you for your concern, but I have another call coming through and they have been trying to reach us since you and I first started talking. Thanks, again. Goodbye." And with that I hung up just as Desmond's cell number showed on the caller ID window.

Desmond explained that they were having trouble setting things up on the computer at his end. Apparently, Windows machines were not able to do 'Facetime' since Apple owned the technology. So, they were moving to another office and would be calling back in a couple minutes. He gave us the phone number that the call would be originated from so we would recognize the call as his.

Stephanie and I decided we had enough time to make a cup of tea and return to my office before Desmond's phone call. We both wondered out loud as to why Sarah Douglas had called, and speculated as to what her plan was. It only took a few more minutes before Desmond's call came through.

"Guys, this is my close friend, Devon Miller," Desmond said as another face appeared onscreen. "Devon is a senior investigator within NSA, and is aware of the info we have on Guido Kiefer, et al." Devon smiled, said hello and showed his badge and identification to us. "Devon would like to accompany me to your house and have a meeting to review the copies of Guido's papers. He would also like to bring another investigator from the State Department's office of International Affairs for the Far East. The FBI is also been made aware of the allegations we could make against Ben Haberman and Sarah Douglas."

"By the way, Desmond" I said, interrupting Desmond's talking, "Just before your last call came through, I was on the phone with Sarah."

"Why were you talking with Sarah?" Desmond quizzed.

"She called us," Stephanie told Desmond. "Playing some sort of fishing game with news about Guido Kiefer's death aboard the Asian Airlines missing plane. She claimed that a friend of hers works at Asian and had given her bad news about some sorority sister of hers who was aboard that plane."

"That's very interesting," Devon Miller said. "We are reviewing the passenger list and getting information concerning all relatives for each passenger. I don't believe there were any passengers who would have been linked in any way to Sarah Douglas, or her sorority. We will cross check sorority members names, also, for confirmation. There were five non-Asian passengers aboard the flight: one American businessman, one businessman from the UK, two French women, and one woman from Madrid, Spain. None of them were members of Sarah's sorority."

"What about the American movie actor?" I asked. "You didn't mention him."

"No American movie actor onboard," Devon said. "Only the one businessman, who we presumed to have been Guido Kiefer." Devon and Desmond talked quietly to each other before Devon asked, "What is this about some American movie actor?"

I explained that a doctor from the hospital in Bangkok had called early this morning saying that the person they had asked me to identify, had finally been identified as an American movie actor named Jim Hanover. They said he was enroute to Myanmar to be part of a movie being filmed there. They said that identification had been confirmed.

"That's very interesting," Devon said raising his eyebrows. "We will get in touch with our local people there and check that out. But, listen, there is so much more that we should, and can, discuss in a face-to-face contact, that should not be discussed in this transmission. Can we get together? Perhaps, even today, or first thing tomorrow morning?"

Stephanie said that she thought the sooner, the better for the meeting. I agreed and told Desmond and Devon that we would make ourselves available anytime they could meet. Devon said he would confirm that State Department personnel were available and be to our house in an hour. If not, he would send a text message to my cell phone.

"An hour? I asked.

Devon chuckled saying "Yes, an hour. This is such a high priority item that we all will 'copter' to your home. Desmond tells me that you have large flat grass lawns where we can land a helicopter. True?"

"True" I answered.

"We'll see you in an hour, or watch for a text message from me. I have your cell phone number." And with that Devon ended the 'Facetime' chat.

Stephanie and I just sat in my office for a few minutes in silence before she said she would go straighten up the family room before they arrived. I suggested that we use the dining room table because of its' roominess, and that room is closer to my office in case we need any of the documents.

We both straightened up a few things, Stephanie dusted slightly, and we both went to our bedroom to change.

It seemed like only ten or fifteen minutes passed and we heard the whirling sound of a helicopter approaching. It took another five minutes before it landed, and the four men were shaking our hands in the front entryway. Devon sort of led the group as to where to sit.

"Are you folks aware that you have people watching you?" the FBI agent asked us.

"What?" I asked. "What do you mean, 'watching us'?"

He took me to the side of the dining room windows and gently pulled back a small piece of drapery. He described in detail an old, grey colored Mercury Marquis parked just down the road beyond our gates. Two men dressed in dark clothing sat in the front seats; one had a camera with a big lens attached. I looked through the small opening he had created to confirm what he was telling us was true. Stephanie became very irritated, and angered at this news. She wanted someone to go arrest them for spying on us.

"I know it's very uncomfortable for you, ma'am, but we need to find out, first, what it is they are up to. We can arrest them at any time, but we need something to charge them with." The FBI agent was right, but it didn't make Stephanie any less angry.

So we all took seats around the dining room table with the FBI guy sitting opposite the windows so he could shoot a glance at the onlookers on occasion. He also called for more agents to get in position to watch the two watching us. Apparently, Westport, Connecticut must have an over-abundance of FBI agents lurking around. Or, the bureau was concentrating resources close by.

We were into our meeting just slightly over two hours when Mr. FBI said that the two people watching our house had just left. He looked down at his lap and texted a message to someone. The Mercury had left with both a drone, and an old panel "Fish Company" truck following them. "Wow!" I thought, are we acting in some sort of movie?

The four men were talking in order of department ranking, I guessed. State Department first, then NSA, then FBI. The fourth man finally identified himself as really being with CIA. He came along because of the foreign government possibly being involved. We didn't know if we should be honored, or not, at having so many government departments focused on us. CIA was also concerned about Sorrabon Corporation, and their acquisition of many U.S. and foreign companies. They had gotten government approval for most of the acquisitions, but not the foreign ones. They were hiding companies within companies within other companies. FBI, among other agencies was watching Sorrabon very closely.

The meeting was well into the dinner hour before Devon asked if anyone had any further questions, or needed to see any of the papers we have, again. After everyone said that they had what they needed, Devon warned Stephanie and I that the Mercury would probably change to some other make, model and color. But be certain that they would continue watching us. If, possible, note the time and date somewhere that we observe them, and FBI would compare our dates and times with theirs.

Everyone thanked us for our help and assistance, shook hands and left for the waiting helicopter. Within a couple minutes, they were lifting off, and disappearing into the light fog coming into the Long Island Sound.

Stephanie suggested we run into town and grab some dinner before be get too involved in analyzing everything that had occurred this afternoon. I wondered if it was safe to leave the house empty after having those people watch us today. Maybe one of us should stay here and have their cell phone ready. I volunteered to go get some Chinese take-out and bring it home, but I was adamant that Stephanie have her cell phone in her hand the entire time I was gone. I also was going to set the alarm to the 'occupied' mode so that anyone who tried to enter without the code would set off the alarm.

I set off in my car for downtown Westport, and Chinese take-out. Driving, paying close attention to other cars, people out walking, and people I could see inside businesses as I passed them. Nothing could prevent me from thinking about today's meeting in our dining room, and what might happen in the days to follow.

What have we gotten ourselves in to?

Several days passed, and still no sign of another auto, or people, watching Stephanie or me. We used binoculars from both the house and the boat, to watch down the road and in other directions less accessible. We had not become paranoid, yet, but the FBI kept texting messages asking about the status of the 'watches.' The 'watches' was the code word set up by Devon and MR. FBI, and the emails always originated from a jewelry store on 47th street in New York City. Pretty clever those FBI people.

Life continued on just like it always had; Stephanie out for her morning jogs, her gardening around our house, both of us working on the boat, and me, only me, going into town for take-out foods. Other than us never leaving the house, everything was 'normal,' whatever normal was.

Life as we were living it was not bad; not bad at all. I enjoyed having Stephanie working from home and the house and grounds never looked better. The boat, even though it was new, had never seen shinier metal components, better kept decks, or cleaner windows. There were distinct advantages to how we were living life.

Nearly four weeks passed before the house phone rang one morning. It was Mr. FBI guy saying he was sending me an email. He gave me a code to use to decipher the phone number that he needed me to use to call him. Without saying any more, he hung up. About three minutes later, four emails came through. One matched the code he had given me and I deciphered the words and numbers to get a phone number. As I picked up my office phone I saw a flash of light shoot across the dining room wall. Curious, I walked into the dining room, looked out the window, and saw an old, Chrysler auto with a lot of primer spots on the body. Two men clothed in dark clothing sat in the front seats.

Without further delay I walked back to the office, dialed the phone number, and heard Devon answer. He explained that things were about to come to a head with everyone. I told him that I had just seen the two guys sitting in a different car down the road to our house. Devon said he was aware of them, and they would be apprehended in about six to seven minutes. Also, they had confirmation that Gilbert Keeper, a.k.a. Guido Kiefer, was still alive and had nearly been caught in a small Arizona town earlier in the week. He got away, but Devon was certain they would catch him. The real news was that they had been working with the U.S. Attorney's office and were about to arrest both Sarah Douglas, and Ben Haberman. There is enough evidence against them to send them to prison for ninety years or more. Devon simply wanted to alert us to where the investigation was, and the timeline for moving forward. Would Stephanie and I be available to meet with him the day after tomorrow, to go over how things will play out? I assured him we would.

After Devon's call ended, I went to the dining room window to look out and see about ten uniformed officers putting handcuffs on the two men. They were quickly ushered into a black, unmarked police van, and within thirty seconds the two men, the ten officers, the black van, and the old primer-covered Chrysler were gone. Not a trace of any of it.

About an hour later, the house phone rang again. This time it was an official from UCONN phoning in regards to me accepting, or not, the professor's position within the literature department. He said that they can set up a meeting with me and department heads to answer any questions that I might have. I told him I would be involved in a matter of national security for the next few days, so I could not give him any answer, yet. He asked if he could call at the end of next week and get my answer, as they must fill the position before long. I set up a day and time that I would make myself available next week. He thanked me for my time and hung up.

I decided to take the boat out for a short cruise. Stephanie was busy in her home office reviewing contracts for a client. She locked herself in there and wanted to get all her work done before the afternoon partner's conference call. Good time to relax and cruise.

Stephanie finished her work before the conference call came through. The senior partner did a quick roll call and then asked Stephanie if she was alone at home, or not. She told him she was completely alone and asked why. It seems that one of Stephanie's partners was a board member of Sorrabon Corporation and needed to have a confidential partners discussion on the subject. He had excused himself from all previous discussions regarding Sorrabon, so this request seemed strange to Stephanie.

The Board of Directors of Sorrabon had been informed of the arrest, and jailing, of Mr. Ben Haberman, and Ms. Sarah Douglas. Both individuals were being charged with somewhere around twenty-two counts of embezzlement, theft, conspiracy to defraud the U.S. Government, and conspiring with a foreign government in matters detrimental to the security of the United States. There were nineteen additional counts charged against Ben, and eleven additional against Sarah. The board had started its' own investigation of the two, and had an outside accounting firm start examining the corporate financials. Their board was going to meet in executive session to elect a new, pro-tem, CEO of Sorrabon, and Stephanie's partner would like to nominate me to fill the president's position at the publishing company. He asked Stephanie how she thought I would react to his plan, and if selected would I be interested. Stephanie asked if this was something she could openly discuss with me when I returned. He said she could, and that the board members would not need to have a decision for another forty-eight hours. The partners then concluded regular business and ended the conference call.

I brought the boat back several hours later and found Stephanie sitting in the family room watching the evening news. The headline story, of course, was all about the arrest of the CEO of Sorrabon Corporation, a major international company with operations throughout the U.S., the UK, Asia, Europe and South America. Also the arrest of the president of one of their major companies, Sorrabon Publishing headquartered here in New York City. Both arrested individuals were being charged with federal crimes and were considered to be flight risks. Therefore no amount of bail had been set.

"Things finally caught up to Ben Haberman and Ms. Sarah," Stephanie told me. "They were arrested this morning and are being held without bail. Since some charges against them involved matters of national security, they will be held in a maximum security jail cell until trial."

Stephanie then told me about the partners' conference call, and how the partner who is on the board of Sorrabon wants to nominate me for the position of president of Sorrabon Publishing. He wonders how I would feel about it if he does and if I am selected. Stephanie asked me if I would accept the position, and I had to tell her I didn't know yet. I would need more information about their plans for the growth of the company, and what they expect the company to contribute to their bottom line, and a myriad of other things.

We sat and watched on-the-street interviews with 'ordinary citizens' about some of the charges filed against Ben and Sarah. We watched the network business gurus speculate about the future of print and digital publishing in this country, and what effect they felt this would have on stocks and the market. We watched in silence as each and every one interviewed on TV had profound, insightful thoughts on how far astray these two 'hardened criminals' had gone. Both Stephanie and I watched in silence and wondered about a myriad of things.

The following day was filled with more 'follow up' news stories about the arrest and jailing of Ben and Sarah; about the record-breaking number of charges that were being filed against both of them and how both the State of New York, and the Federal government attorneys were licking their lips with the amount of evidence against them. All this was more of what had already been discussed, re-discussed, analyzed, and analyzed over, again.

I planned to spend the day doing research for data to construct my next story line, while Stephanie was reviewing contracts for clients, as well as making phone calls to clients throughout the day.

I also decided to make an additional copy of everything of Guido's that we had, so that both the NSA and FBI could have an entire 'set' of copies of data for their respective uses. Making that many additional copies would be a time consuming project and making copies of data-filled CD's would add more time to it. It was not any matter of distrust of government people that prompted me to make more copies, it was my internal desire to NEVER lose important bits of information.

As evening approached, Stephanie asked if it would be possible for us to get out of the house and go out for dinner, rather than getting "something take-out." She told me about some restaurants that clients had recommended to her, ranging from Mexican food all the way to Japanese-Peruvian fusion cuisine. It was her question that suddenly reminded me how long it had been since she had been out of the house; especially for a dinner. Other than her morning jogs, she had been bound to our property, not even aboard the "Stephanie's Joy" for cruising.

The more Stephanie talked about the Japanese-Peruvian fusion restaurant in Norwalk, the more intriguing it sounded. She had made notes regarding it so that we could look it up on the internet sometime if we ever wanted to give it a try. Named "Aji 10" Latin cuisine and Pisco bar, it was easy to find online, and located downtown Norwalk. The online menu had both our mouths watering as we read dish-after-dish-after-dish. It became a really easy sell and we decided to go clean up and take a drive to Norwalk.

The drive down the turnpike was easy and seemed to lack the 'normal' amount of commute traffic. We found the 'Aji 10', on Wall Street, easily enough. Parking was not a major problem for a restaurant located on a 'traffic round-about'. Deciding what each of us would eat was a problem, but, after lengthy consideration we both decided to try something different from each other.

Dinner was excellent and both Stephanie and I vowed to come back again for dinner; really soon. We went for a walk about the area before retrieving the car and heading home. It had been a really nice evening, and a special treat for Stephanie just getting out of the house. We laughed about how 'crazy' our lives had become since the Asian Airlines missing plane incident. We joked about how things had gone from bad, to worse, to better, to great for me and how Stephanie had been able to increase business for her law firm, even in spite of everything else that was going on.

I parked my car in the garage and we took a walk down to the pier to marvel at the full moon and how it played on the water in the river. Some boaters were making their way slowly down the river toward the Long Island Sound. Maybe some were fellow club members and just out for an enjoyable spring-like evening of cruising.

CHAPTER 15

As we watched everything, we both got a very faint whiff of that stomach-turning, sickening aroma of decaying meat. We looked at each other and asked the other if we were actually smelling something, or just our imaginations working overtime.

We looked around but nothing was different. Stephanie asked me if the smell could be coming from the boat. I told her that there was not any meat on the boat, nor was there anything that would spoil. We only had 'packaged', non-perishable food onboard, so I doubted that the sickening smell was coming from the boat. As it got stronger, we decided to try to escape it and head for the house to check emails and phone messages.

I didn't remember the umbrella falling onto the floor when we left, but there it was now just laying there in the rear entryway. I picked it up and hung it back on one of the coat hooks. Stephanie asked me if I wanted a cup of tea as she was going to make some for herself. I thought that sounded like a good idea as I still had a few more things to finish to get ready for our meeting with Devon and Desmond tomorrow. I told her I would be in my office working and just to give a shout when it was ready.

I got involved going through the fifty-odd emails that had accumulated during the day. While I absolutely love the internet, especially when it becomes necessary for me to do research, I detest the flood of emails that people can send that are absolutely unwanted by the recipients. But, they wouldn't clear themselves out, so I started in. Amazing how many totally useless creations filled up my email inbox. One-after-another-after-another seemed to have been a huge waste of time for someone, but I gradually got the bunch cleared out. What happened to the tea, I wondered, as I practiced yet another big yawn.

"Hey, Stephanie," I called out to her, "need some help with the tea?" There was that damn sickening odor again. Seemed to be coming from the floor, the walls, the ceiling, everywhere. If it got any stronger, it could drive us out of the house. How was sleeping going to be possible tonight?

"Stephanie?" I called out. No response. I walked toward the kitchen as the odor became stronger; my stomach was telling me that there was a real contest about to happen between the odor and my ability to keep dinner down.

As I walked into the kitchen I heard a click sound. A short, distinct metallic click sound and looked to see Stephanie bound, and unconscious , in a kitchen chair. There holding a rather large gun pointed directly at Stephanie's temple was Guido Kiefer. The man 'presumed dead and missing' was certainly alive and not missing. Whatever Guido had done to Stephanie, whatever Guido wanted from us, he definitely had my attention.

"Good evening" he said. "Sorry I didn't call first but I thought a surprise visit might work out better for all of us, especially me"

"What did you do to her?" I yelled at Guido as I slowly raised my arms upward. I could see that Stephanie was still breathing but beyond that I had no clue as to what her physical condition was.

"Nothing that a short nap won't cure." He said. Guido used the gun to motion for me to move over to my right. He then told me to sit down in the vacant chair and put both arms behind me.

"And if I don't?" I asked, trying to show some resistance to his demand.

"I have nothing to lose by killing you both!" Guido answered. "I'm already dead, so you can't kill me twice. Now SIT DOWN!"

I did as he told me to do and had my hands and arms tied securely with some rope from the garage. That's what was out of place, I thought. When I parked the car in the garage earlier, I noticed that some tools and things were laying on the workbench area. Something I prided myself in, among other things, was that I always cleaned up and straightened up after I was done. Funny I didn't pay more attention to that one thing.

Guido continued telling me all about the plane flight from Singapore to Myanmar that never landed there, but did make a crash landing in the Adaman Sea just off the coast of Phang Nga, Thailand. He talked about how he was unconscious before coming to on a beach somewhere in Thailand. He got help from locals, and was eventually able to find out that he was supposedly in critical condition in some hospital in Bangkok. He followed his story until they determined that he had died, or was among the missing passengers. By then, he was in better health and was able to travel.

Seems Guido was hell-bent on getting his share of any money that Ben and Sarah had stolen and stashed away for a long time. He found a village where some Catholic missionaries were doing their 'thing' to save the world. He found a priest that was about the same size and general physical description as Guido, so Guido killed the priest and took his clothes and passport. He continued his travels back to the U.S. and had been watching Stephanie and I through a high-powered telescope from the trees on the other side of the river. He knew all about the group of 'serious-looking' men in dark suits that had been here having a meeting. He knew that Ben, or Sarah had a couple men watching us from down the road, and he knew that at any time, he could break into our house and get what he needed. What he didn't know was that the Federal government would have so much information on Ben and Sarah and would arrest them so soon, holding them in federal jail without bail. That he didn't understand, but he knew when that happened that he had better move fast.

As Guido talked, the raunchy, rotting meat odor kept getting stronger and stronger. At one point Guido stopped talking, took a smell, and said we really needed to clean out our refrigerator of old hamburger.

I asked Guido what it was that was in this house that he needed so badly that he would do this to us. Guido just laughed and said that he would answer that question when he 'found' it. With that he noticed Stephanie returning to consciousness, and laughed as he said "good morning" to her. He walked around in front of us, grabbed her hair and yanked her head upright. He told me that he had given her a little smell of something to put her to sleep and she would be fine in a few more minutes. Seems as though Guido learned a lot from the 'locals' while in Thailand.

Guido left for several minutes only to return with more rope which he used to secure our legs to our chairs. After checking all his knots, and such, he said he would be busy for a while, but would be looking in on us every few minutes. If we behaved ourselves, and did what he asked, we would live; otherwise, he would not hesitate a second to kill us both. I thought to myself that the next time I choose groomsmen, I would think a lot longer before choosing another Guido.

He had also brought back with him several tools including a crowbar and long pry rod. I wondered what all the tools would be used for but was not about to ask. Guido went off upstairs to do whatever it was that he wanted to do.

In the meantime I whispered to Stephanie to see if she was awake, or not. She whispered back she was but did not want to show Guido too much for fear that he would get mad and shoot us. She asked if I had a plan; to which I giggled saying that I wished I did, but not yet. She told me that Guido was hiding in the kitchen and when she walked in to start our tea water, that he grabbed her putting something over her mouth and nose, and injecting her in her arm. Seconds later she was out like a light.

Throughout the night we heard noise coming from various parts of the upstairs' rooms. Sometimes very loud, sometimes barely hearable. Every once in awhile the noise sounded like Guido was busy removing walls from a room. It went on for hours and hours with Guido poking his nose into the kitchen to check on us every so often.

"You two play nice with each other," he joked at one point, "While I play with my tools upstairs."

The sun had risen and bright light was filling every room in the house. I was so curious as to what Guido was looking for, but not about to ask.

Around nine-thirty in the morning, he stopped tearing things apart and came into the kitchen to make himself some coffee. "Just love these Keurig machines, don't you?" he asked. He brewed himself a cup of my dark roast and started laughing. "My, o my! How I bet you two would love to have a cup of coffee, but, you see, you can't hold a cup! And, I'm not going to hold it for you. Either one of you." With that, he took off back up the stairway.

I had been busy trying to come up with some form of escape plan but the more I wriggled in my chair the more securely we seemed to be tied. I could not come up with any ideas, even though in book six of my novels, my hero had done something like this and escaped. Not in this reality.

About an hour-and-a-half later, Guido, looking very exhausted and sweating a lot, came back into the kitchen. He said that what he was looking for was not to be found on the third, or the second floors. He was betting that it was somewhere in the basement because he knew that his grandfather would not hide valuables on the first floor.

He double checked our ropes and knots before heading off for the basement.

It's funny how the simplest things become very, very annoying when you can't do them, or do them properly. While being bound to the chairs, dust really, I mean REALLY irritated our noses and we could not do anything about it. No bathroom breaks, either, which strained endurance to the breaking point. Scratching an itch was just not possible. Ever have an itch when you couldn't scratch it? Terrible!

We sat whispering to each other when suddenly Stephanie stopped. What was wrong, now? I asked her. She told me that she thought she saw a face outside the dining room window. I told her it was probably Guido continuing his search outside. She said that it definitely wasn't Guido's face, but she didn't know who it was.

Minutes later, Guido came into the kitchen without any tools. He had his rather large gun in his hand, again, and was pointing it at Stephanie.

"I guess that you two have already found the 'stash' of things I'm looking for" Guido said, waving his gun back and forth. He seemed to be getting more anxious and agitated as the minutes passed. He pointed the gun directly at my head and asked, "where did you put it?"

Not knowing what Guido was referring to, I was hesitant to answer. He pulled the hammer of the gun back which made that same metallic click sound I had heard last night. Guido asked me again where I had put his things as the barrel of the cold metal gun was pressed against my forehead.

"Honest, Guido," I said, "I have no idea what you are talking about. If I did I would tell you where, but we don't have anything of yours. What are you looking for?"

For a moment Guido looked deep into my eyes and I thought he might just pull the trigger. After about twenty seconds, which seemed like an hour, he released the gun's hammer and took a step back. He continued to look at me when suddenly he did an 'about face' and pointed the gun at Stephanie.

"You're not afraid to die," Guido said, "but I bet you wouldn't like what a bullet from this gun would do to your lovely wife." He never took his eyes off of me as he pulled the gun hammer back, once more. His hand, which had to this moment been firm and very steady, was now beginning to tremble a bit. "Do you know how much splatter there would be in this kitchen from her head as one bullet rips it into so many little, little pieces?"

I was at a loss for words at this point because he didn't seem to hear, or not believe what I was telling him about his things.

"Guido," I said, "you can kill us both if you want but we can't tell you where something is when we don't know."

With a very trembling, weak voice, Stephanie said, "I may know." Guido looked around at her and moved the gun away from her face.

"What do you mean that you may know?" I asked her.

"The electrical contractor found three metal boxes, and a larger metal case with combination locks on it, somewhere in the basement when he was installing the additional lights down there. He gave them to me, and I put them on the upper shelf in the third garage." Stephanie's voice had gotten slightly stronger. "I meant to mention them to you, but forgot all about them. They are still out there, I would guess. I don't know if they are what you're looking for, Guido, but they are the only thing that has been found here since we've moved in." It was now that I noticed that Stephanie had been working her hands back and forth in trying to get out of her binding ropes. She had worked them back and forth so much that her wrists were starting to bleed, and little droplets of blood were beginning to drop on the kitchen floor.

"Upper shelf in garage three?" asked Guido. "I'll have myself a look."

With that, Guido made his way out the back door without saying another word.

I told Stephanie that her wrists were starting to bleed and she was getting blood on the floor. She said she thought so and was only able to loosen her ties slightly. She said her wrists and hands were beginning to throb in pain and she didn't know if

184

she would be able to loosen them any more, or not. I also asked her if she was telling Guido the truth or not. She said she was telling the truth and apologized for forgetting to tell me about them. I told her not to worry about it.

It only took Guido five or six minutes to retrieve the three metal boxes and the larger metal case, and return to the kitchen. As he was trying to set all of them on the counter, the sickening aroma of decaying meat started to permeate throughout the area. Guido ignored the odor and looked at the metal locks on each box. The odor continued to gain in strength as we watched Guido examine each lock. Realizing he needed either a key, or some type of pry tool, he started opening kitchen drawers to search for one. About this time a low, soulful, moaning sound emanated upward from below the kitchen floor. The odor kept getting stronger and more putrid by the minute.

Guido failed to find anything satisfactory in the drawers in the kitchen island, so he asked if I had a crowbar, or big pry bar any where. I told him that all tools were above the workbench in the first garage area and there should be something there. I pleaded with Guido to open a door or some windows before Stephanie, or I, got sick to our stomach.

It's really getting to me, also," Guido told me, "but if I kill you both right now, then you won't have anything to worry about. Now shut up and hold your breath!" With that, Guido left the kitchen, again, and went to the garage.

The odor continued to worsen; it got stronger and seemed to just take our breath away. We both started to breathe through our mouths in short, quick breaths. Our eyes were becoming very irritated by the pungent odor, and tears were both forming and running down our cheeks. The moaning was becoming louder and more audible, also.

As Guido re-entered the kitchen with a crowbar, there was a low rumbling sound all around us. This sound was accompanied by some vibrating of the ground and house. Guido ignored everything completely and just focused on opening the boxes. The vibrating turned into more of a rumbling and shaking and kept increasing in intensity. Guido only focused on prying the top of the first metal box open as rumbling increased and increased. The horrendous odor was getting so obnoxious that both Stephanie and I were gagging off and on. I pleaded with Guido to please open some windows and doors to bring fresher air inside. He ignored my pleas and tried to pry open another metal box without success.

As Guido worked on opening the metal box, things began to get violent. We were having an earthquake with the house shaking violently, kitchen cabinet doors swung open, and both Stephanie and my chairs were being bounced around the kitchen as if we were dancing with them. Guido was having difficulty both standing, and holding onto the box and his tools.

I thought the house was going to come apart completely as the shaking increased. Along with all the shaking, the odor kept getting worse, and the moaning had turned into a loud, gruesome groaning sound. It kept on, and on. Several minutes passed and nothing decreased, either in loudness, or intensity of shaking. The pungent odor was sickening and both Stephanie, Guido and I were gasping for air trying to breathe. I knew we were about to pass out for lack of breathable air, but nothing was ending. Our misery just went on. The horrendous shaking caused Guido to loose his balance often and stumble around just trying to stand upright.

Suddenly, there was a rush of cool, fresh air as several men dressed in dark clothing rushed into the kitchen yelling "get down! Get down! Do not attempt to move!" They grabbed onto Guido, while some other men seem to tackle him and Guido hit the floor with a loud 'THUD!'

His yelling and cussing went unnoticed as the men, not dealing with Guido on the floor, rushed over to Stephanie and I to cut our ropes and check on our well being. One man held a radio of some sort into which he yelled "Medic! Medic! One hostage injured, we need a medic, immediately!" So much was going on simultaneously, that it became mostly a blur of non-distinguishable images moving about our kitchen. Before I knew it, I was on my feet being carried out through the back door to the patio where Stephanie was already being looked at by a medic and a nurse.

A few minutes later Guido was brought out the back door in handcuffs and leg chains. He was still yelling obscenities at everyone handling him and even took time to spit on one fellow. He was forced to sit on a patio chair and told to shut up. As my eyes began to clear up, and my vision cleared, I could make out the number and size of the men in black. One man walked over to Guido and put a black hood over his head.

After that, all the men removed their masks and straightened their hair. One man I recognized as Devon, but the others were all strangers. Devon put his index finger to his lips to tell Stephanie and I to be quiet and not talk.

Less than a minute later a large, black, unmarked van pulled up in the driveway. Several men took Guido by his arms and ushered him into the back of the van, and closed the rear doors. Devon told us that we could now talk openly as the van was soundproof inside. He explained that when he and Desmond arrived this morning for our update meeting, that they saw an old man sort of peeking into our windows. When they stopped this man at the gates, he told them what he had seen going on inside. With that information Devon called for backup and a special FBI hostage squad.

It took awhile before they had full understanding of what was happening and could begin to put together a suitable rescue plan. Also, while this planning was going on, the house seemed to be having a violent earth quake with shaking, moving, and lots of sound effects going on. It was only at this point that I noticed that everything had stopped. The odor was gone. The moaning, and all other sound effects had ended, and, probably the most noticeable, the earthquake ended! Everything that was going on while Guido was keeping them hostage, had ended.

Devon said that they were getting lots of information about Guido Kiefer from Sarah Douglas, and that the bureau was not convinced that Guido was dead. Missing? Yes, but not necessarily dead. Sarah had checked into Guido's background and family before making him help her and Ben Haberman steal a fortune from their employers. Seemed that Sarah knew more than enough about Guido's family to blackmail him and make him 'cook' the books to cover their thefts.

Devon also said that apparently, Guido Kiefer, rather Gilbert Keeper has two sisters and a younger brother. All four siblings know of the murder of the Keeper family and each one has bits of evidence that tell who the murderer is. They have all disappeared except for Gilbert, who chose to stay fairly local and not hide out of state with an alias. An older sister is rumored to be somewhere around here. The bureau has not located her yet, Devon said, but they will. They want to corral all four of them and get all the pieces of the murder puzzle put together. He told us that they would be taking Gilbert off to the federal prison to be held until his trial, and that we would be called as witnesses.

Before the group drove away, the medics made certain that we were okay and that the house had been checked out, top to basement, to be sure everything was okay. One medic said that there appeared to be extensive surface damage done to most walls and some ceilings. Whatever Gilbert was looking for, he was emphatic in his efforts to locate it; to the point of destroying just about everything he could.

After everyone left, both Stephanie and I just sat in quiet solitude without saying anything to each other. We simply listened to the sound of silence and our own thoughts. After ten minutes, or so, we both decided to shower and change clothes. Then we might think about some food. Think about it, hell! We both were starved and needed to eat!

CHAPTER 16

It had been three months since the 'rescue' had occurred, and most of the walls in the house had been repaired. Whatever else Gilbert Keeper had done, he did a masterful job on destroying interior walls. The contractor we hired was not able to match some of the paint colors, so Stephanie had fun choosing new wall paint colors. Moldings have been replaced and only a few items which had to be special ordered have yet to be installed. Gradually, Stephanie told me one morning at breakfast, our lives and our home were being put back in order. The boat helped us both to live 'outside' the house while the work went on. We even spent eleven nights onboard "Stephanie's Joy" when things were really bad.

The trials were interesting. Ben Haberman ended up being charged with sixty seven different counts and was found guilty on forty one of them. His sentence in federal prison totals one-hundred-sixty-one years, but Ben can be eligible for parole after one-hundred-eighteen years. He was also found guilty on sixteen State of New York charges and would spend an additional seventy-five years in state prison when paroled from federal prison.

Sarah Douglas, on the other hand, tried to 'cut a deal' with prosecutors to get a lesser sentence, but only the State of New York was willing to discuss such a deal with her attorneys. She tried to turn state's evidence against Ben Haberman, but no one was interested in her information. She has just gone to federal prison to serve her thirty eight consecutive ten year sentences. She is eligible for parole after two-hundred-forty years. She also has been found guilty on eighteen State of New York charges.

I attended Ben's trial, but had to testify in Sarah's. Not something I wanted to do, but when duty calls, it calls. The trials brought out a lot of information about how things started getting out of hand, and how it got worse as it went forward. The notes that Guido, I mean Gilbert, had kept were devastating when used against both Sarah and Ben. Gilbert's fastidious note taking and record keeping was a testament to his ability, to keep accurate records; good, clean, understandable accurate records. Both in print, as well as in digital form Gilbert's information was superlative. Unless, it was being used against you.

Gilbert Keeper also tried to cut a deal to lessen the federal charges he was facing. He brought up his knowledge of all of Sorrabon's subsidiaries, and their methods of hiding U.S. dollars in offshore banks, and such. He said he had a list of each account and its' location, but no one had any real interest in giving Gilbert a chance at a shorter term in prison.

Gilbert's trial has just concluded, and he will also die in federal prison. He was found guilty on every count upon which he was charged. His total years in prison will total one-hundred-ninety-seven years without the possibility of parole. His involvement with the government of China is still under investigation. He could still be brought to trial on national security matters.

I had the opportunity to ask Gilbert, or Guido, what was he looking for the night he tore our house apart. At first he refused to tell me, or answer any of our questions. Finally, after the verdicts came in Gilbert told me that he was looking for vital, important documents that either his grandfather, or father had hidden somewhere in the structure of the house. Documents which included the deeds to homes in Indiana, New Mexico, Colorado and Oregon. In addition, deeds to acreage in Oregon and Utah were among the documents, also. All of this property, now, represented close to twenty-one-million dollars in value. Money that he wanted to start a new life.

I told him that I had forced one of the smaller metal boxes open, only to find love letters from WW1, and a handful of postcards.

His disappointment was quite obvious when he broke down and started crying, shielding his face in his hands. He said that all he ever wanted was to find these missing documents and share with his siblings. He never wanted to cheat anyone, never wanted to help anyone steal money, and he certainly never wanted to be dealing with a foreign government who, on their best day, was still a very suspicious partner of the U.S.

We never got a good, understandable explanation about what had happened with our house. Why did the horrendous odor suddenly appear? Why did the moaning happen? How did the earthquake-like-shaking and rumbling occur? And, what made all of it stop? The discussions ran the range of, "you probably were in a heightened state of frenzy, and just imagined those things," to one paranormal scientist's opinion that, "the house is still possessed by the Keeper Family's spirit, and it tries to protect you whenever it senses that you are in danger." In between, were many, many more opinions and no facts. No one seemed able to explain anything, not even the FBI agents who witnessed it, nor the police officers that were also present during the 'events.' To this day we do not know if we own a house possessed by the spirit of the murdered Keeper family, or if we have a house that is a keeper house of us.

Stephanie went back to work on her regular schedule. She commutes to New York City for meetings with clients, partners' meetings, and, of course, any day she has to be in court. She feels really good and her wrists have healed without leaving any scars. She absolutely loves her little gardens and spends a lot of time giving them her TLC. She also has become quite a good pilot for the "Stephanie's Joy."

I have given UCONN my thanks for the honor of being considered qualified to teach literature at the university. I turned down their offer after much discussion with Stephanie, and much soul searching. I decided that what they were offering was a very good offer, but I did not want to be driving from Westport to Mansfield where the campus is located. Even though the drive was only an hour-and-a-half to two hours, during winter months, it could be murderous.

I also told Marathon Media that I would not be signing to publish with them, as I had accepted an offer to run Sorrabon Publishing. The new corporate board made it clear to me that they wanted me with my creativity and management style to take over Sorrabon Publishing and create an environment that other creative writers would like. Profits were important, of course, but not at the risk of losing talented, creative authors. They felt the company needed a writer to handle and attract writers. They virtually gave me cart blanche to bring the publishing firm back to life. I am putting together a management team of energetic, talented people whom I can trust to get the job done. I am working in the downtown office three days a week and from home the other two. Pretty much the same 'in-town' schedule as Stephanie has developed. We ride the train into downtown together, we ride the train home together, and we take the "Stephanie's Joy" out on the water together.

Yes, life is pretty much "A OK."